TANGLED WEB

After his beloved great-uncle has an angina attack, Jarrett tells his fiancée, Emily, that the elderly man's one wish is to live long enough to see him happily married. Emily agrees to bring their wedding forward but she's devastated when, on their honeymoon, she hears of a clause in Jarrett's great-uncle's will: the first baby boy born in the family will inherit the family business. Has Jarrett only married her so he can produce an heir before either of his brothers beat him to it?

PAT POSNER

TANGLED WEB

Complete and Unabridged

LINFORD
Leicester

First published in Great Britain

First Linford Edition
published 2015

Copyright © 2015 by Pat Posner
All rights reserved

*A catalogue record for this book is available
from the British Library.*

ISBN 978–1–4448–2407–0

Published by
F. A. Thorpe (Publishing)
Anstey, Leicestershire

Set by Words & Graphics Ltd.
Anstey, Leicestershire
Printed and bound in Great Britain by
T. J. International Ltd., Padstow, Cornwall

This book is printed on acid-free paper

1

The bell on Flowerbunch's shop door pinged and Emily, ready with the welcoming smile she used for customers, glanced round from arranging a Valentine's Day display. But when she saw it was her fiancé who'd walked in she threw off that persona and, abandoning the paper hearts and flowers, hurried towards him. 'Jarrett. What a lovely surprise.'

Her mind flickered back to the weekend when he'd come over to Portsmouth so they could spend time together before his business trip. 'You said you'd have to stay up in London 'til Saturday. It's only Tuesday,' she added, staring at him in delight.

How she loved his craggy features — his forehead, with the lock of hair flopping over it as usual, his neat, beautifully shaped eyebrows, the tiny crow's feet at the outer edges of eyes as dark as the night sky, his slightly crooked nose, his mouth . . .

Wait a minute. Jarrett wasn't smiling back at her. His lips seemed tightly compressed — his mouth had a downward curve. 'Is something wrong?' she asked. 'Did some of the buyers cancel?' She knew something like that would upset or annoy him. Nursery World, the business he ran with his two brothers and their great-uncle on the Isle of Wight, was already successful but Jarrett wanted more London outlets for their traditional nursery furniture, play equipment and the range of clothes for babies and toddlers.

'The buyers didn't cancel. I did,' he said. 'Ginny phoned me at my hotel this morning.'

'Your great-uncle's carer? Oh Jarrett, what's happened?'

'Great-unc had an angina attack late last night. He's in hospital and the specialist is a bit concerned.' Jarrett's brows met in scowl. 'The old boy is eighty-five, you know and, although he only comes into the works a couple of days a week, he still keeps a finger on the pulse of his rental properties. The specialist has been ordering him to retire completely for years but even after being so ill last Christmas, Great-unc carried on as usual.'

'Maybe he'll take this as a last warning and do as the specialist says,' Emily suggested.

'That's if he hasn't left it too late,' Jarrett replied. 'But I'm catching the twelve forty-five ferry over and, if he's well enough, I'm going to have a really serious talk with him about taking things a lot easier. I'll get Simon our family doctor and one of my best friends to back me up.'

Emily glanced at her watch. 'You've got time for a coffee,' she said. 'I'll take an early lunch break. Veronica's in the prep room making Valentine's tussie-mussies. A romantic name for bouquets,' she added, seeing Jarrett's puzzled expression. 'We use the language of flowers to decide which flowers to put in the bouquets. For Valentine's Day the meaning of every flower has something to do with love. Anyway, I'll tell Veronica to call me if she needs me and we'll go up to the flat.'

'I was hoping you'd suggest coffee. Nobody makes coffee like you.' Jarrett smiled and gave her a quick hug but Emily could see his thoughts where elsewhere.

After settling Jarrett comfortably in the lounge and telling him to relax, Emily hurried into the kitchen. She knew he wouldn't relax, though. She knew only too well what it felt like to be worried about a loved one.

Two years previously, her mother had contracted a mysterious disease of the muscles, causing loss of leg movement. The specialists, whilst unable to cure her, had managed to arrest the disease. But the Kingstons' large family home wasn't suitable for a wheelchair user, and eventually they decided to move to a bungalow on the Isle of Wight. Emily had gone with them to look at it.

Now, as she busied herself in the

kitchen making a few sandwiches for Jarrett as well as the coffee, Emily dreamily re-lived what had happened next. Jarrett had been the one to show them around the bungalow — one of his great-uncle's properties — and the very first second she'd seen him Emily had known he matched the picture she carried in her heart: her image of her dream man. And as the day went on, she'd known it was more, much more. She'd known he was her soulmate.

Jarrett had clearly felt the same because he'd asked if he could take her out when he came over to the mainland. Two months and a week after their first meeting, on New Year's Eve, he'd proposed and they'd set the wedding date for August 31st — which was Emily's birthday.

Emily gazed lovingly at her engagement ring as she placed everything on a tray before hurrying back to Jarrett, feeling slightly guilty for losing herself in happy memories while the man she loved was sitting here worried sick

5

about his great-uncle.

'Would you like me to come over with you?' she asked, setting the tray down on a small table close to Jarrett's chair. 'We are busy with it being Valentine's Day on Saturday but I could phone Lynne and ask her to swap our hours round.' Lynne, who was married and had two teenage children, was co-manager along with Emily; they split their working hours between them.

'It's a tempting thought,' said Jarrett, 'but I doubt the hospital would allow more than one visitor. Besides, Great-unc put off meeting you that time he'd pulled a neck muscle — didn't want you to see him wearing a neck support, so it would really dent his pride if the first time you see him is when he's in a hospital bed.'

Emily nodded. 'He wouldn't like me hearing you telling him he must start taking things easier, either. That's if he isn't too ill for a lecture,' she added.

'I'm hoping the specialist is more concerned about the future than the present,' Jarrett said. 'So as long as the old boy isn't in immediate danger I'll be coming back later tomorrow. He'll only fret and make himself worse if he thinks I'm missing too many appointments in London.'

'You could spend the night here and take the early train to London on Thursday morning,' Emily suggested.

Jarrett picked up a sandwich and took a huge bite. 'Mmm, nice,' he mumbled. Emily wasn't sure if he meant the thought of them being together the following evening or if he was referring to the sandwich. But when he'd finished that sandwich and another two and smiled across at her, she had her answer. 'The sandwiches were nice, too,' he said. 'I didn't realise how hungry I was.'

There was no time left for any more small talk. Jarrett gulped down the remainder of his coffee and stood up. 'I'll just use the bathroom, then I'm off,' he said.

Emily nodded and watched him walk

towards the door, enjoying the sensation it gave her. His dark hair almost touched the collar of his pale blue silk shirt; the superbly cut navy suit enhanced the broadness of his shoulders and emphasised the length of his legs. And he looked just as good, if not better, in the more casual clothes he wore when he wasn't on a business trip.

Emily's toes curled. She really, really hoped Jarrett would be able to return tomorrow. Not *only* because she couldn't wait for them to be together again, she told herself quickly, but also because if Jarrett did come back the next day, it would mean his great-uncle was well enough to leave.

After she'd seen Jarrett off, Emily, with the memory of his farewell kiss still on her lips and in her heart, told Veronica to take her lunch break. 'I'll finish arranging the Valentine's display,' she said.

★ ★ ★

8

Tuesday afternoons weren't usually busy. But today Emily and Veronica were almost run off their feet with the constant demand for Valentine's tussie-mussies.

'I thought I'd made too many,' Veronica said, shaking her head. 'But there's only three left. I'll come in early tomorrow, Emily, and make a few more.'

'That'd be great, Veronica. Thank you.' Emily smiled and thought, not for the first time, what a lucky choice she and Lynne had made when they'd taken Veronica on straight out of college where she'd had a two-year training course in floristry. The younger girl had been with them for over a year now. Emily and Lynne agreed that she'd be offered Emily's position in August.

Emily would be leaving when she got married; she'd be living in Jarrett's home on the Isle of Wight and didn't fancy ferry travel every day. They'd talked about having children and had both happily decided they wanted to start a family as quickly as possible. If she suffered from morning sickness a ferry ride certainly wouldn't be pleasant.

'Shall I pop into the downstairs kitchen and make us a quick cup of tea?' said Veronica, interrupting Emily's thoughts of the future, the vision of three or four little daughters or sons crowding round the newest baby. 'It's almost five o'clock; I don't suppose we'll get many more customers now.'

'Make it quick and big,' Emily replied. 'My throat's as dry as our lavender and marigold potpourri.'

Veronica laughed and hurried off and Emily began to tidy up. After taking what remained of the cut flowers through to the prep room for the night, she was just about to sweep the floor when the shop door opened and a tall redhead walked in. 'You must be Emily,' she said with a friendly smile. 'Big hazel eyes and a long brown plait, just like Jarrett described you.'

Emily must have looked as puzzled as

she felt because the redheaded woman smiled again, then said, 'I'm Maria, Jarrett's cousin. His mother and mine were sisters.'

'Oh, right,' Emily said, smiling back. 'Jarrett has mentioned you. You've got a theatrical supply business in Chichester.'

'That's right. And seeing as it takes less than half an hour to get here, it's disgusting I haven't come to visit you sooner. I did mean to,' Maria said, wrinkling her nose, 'but, well, you know how it goes when you're running a business. Staff go off sick or take a holiday, you get an urgent order or some other emergency crops up.'

'Touch wood,' Emily said and touched the handle of the broom she'd propped against the counter, 'we don't get too many problems like that. But I know what you mean. Business *can* get in the way of social life.'

'Today I'm hoping the business side of things has allowed me a bit of social life,' Maria said. 'I'm on my way to the

King's Theatre in Southsea to see the props manager. It won't take long and I'll be free for the evening. The social part of it's down to you, Emily. I know Jarrett's in London — his sister-in-law told me when she phoned a couple of days ago. But if you haven't arranged anything with him, I wondered if you'd like to come for a meal?'

After explaining to Maria about Jarrett going back to Wight, Emily said she'd be delighted to go for a meal.

Veronica arrived with two huge mugs of tea just in time to hear that last remark. 'You ought to go to the Mexican restaurant where my boyfriend and I went last week when we were flat-hunting,' she said after Emily introduced her to Jarrett's cousin.

'I love Mexican food,' said Maria.

'Me too,' Emily agreed. 'It probably won't be busy on a Tuesday but shall I phone and make sure we can get a table?'

Maria nodded. 'About eight-ish, if that's all right for you.'

And after Emily had booked the table Maria whirled out, leaving behind her a hint of perfume that mingled pleasantly with the scent from the flowers.

'We'd better drink the tea straight down and then get the tidying-up finished quickly,' Veronica said. 'You'll want time for a long soak before you get ready to go out. What are you wearing? You won't want anything too bright or you'll clash with Maria. I'd never have thought red, blue and green would suit someone with red hair.'

Emily grinned as she reached once more for the broom. 'She is a bit flamboyant, isn't she? It sort of matches her personality, though. I think I'll settle for my long, pale turquoise skirt, a white top and that turquoise lacy bolero shawl you bought me for Christmas.'

'Sounds good,' said Veronica. 'And I'm coming in early in the morning, remember, so don't bother about being down for the flower delivery. You don't want to be rushing over your meal because of needing to get to bed early so you can get up in time for the flower lorry.'

'Hey, I know I'm older than you but twenty-five isn't exactly ancient,' Emily protested laughingly. 'I'm not past burning the candle at both ends yet, you know. But, thank you, Veronica, it'll be good knowing I don't have to crawl out of bed at an unearthly hour if I don't feel up to it.'

After that, they finished tidying everything and by six-thirty, Emily was running the water for a good, hot, deep soak. She was looking forward to her evening out. Apart from meeting William, Jarrett's older brother, very briefly, she hadn't met Jarrett's other brother or any of his other relations yet. And she hadn't met any of Jarrett's friends, either. Well, she had met and liked Mrs Benson, who was Jarrett's motherly housekeeper. But, along with Maria, that was it.

Jarrett talks enthusiastically about Nursery World and his favourite places on *Wight, but he's never talked much about when he was young, or even about more recent times before we met,* Emily thought as she swished some floral bath salts around in the bath water. *I'll get Maria to tell me about Jarrett when he was little and about his family and friends.*

★   ★   ★

'So,' said Maria, after she and Emily made their selections from the menu, 'you and Jarrett met last October when you went to look over one of his great-uncle's properties. What made you decide you wanted to live on the Isle of Wight?'

Emily explained about her mother's illness and the search for a more suitable place to live. 'But at that point in time I wasn't thinking of moving. It was just going to be my parents, along with my younger sisters. They're twelve, thirteen and fourteen.'

'How do they feel about the move?'

Maria asked. 'I was twelve when my aunt and uncle died and I was devastated when Mum told me we were moving to their house because she thought it better not to uproot my cousins.'

'Clair, Abigail and Sara are counting the days,' said Emily. 'They love the island, they adore the bungalow, and the boarding school there has accepted them as weekly boarders. The work on the bungalow — things to make it easier for a wheelchair user — should be finished by the end of next month. The move is planned for then and my sisters will start school after Easter. They can't believe their dream of going to a boarding school is coming true.'

'And them going to boarding school will make it easier for your mum.' Maria nodded.

'For Dad, too,' Emily said. 'Neither Mum nor Dad wanted my sisters to miss out on everything girls of their age usually do; they didn't want them having to rely solely on public transport or lifts from friends' parents for getting to and from school, either. Dad gave up work so he was always there if he was needed. Well, that's the reason he gave. I think really, he was always scared Mum would have a relapse and he wanted to be around to make sure she didn't over-do things.'

Emily picked up her glass of mineral water and swirled the slice of lemon around. She didn't like remembering those early days after her mother had come home. They'd all been frightened of letting her do anything — until, eventually Mrs Kingston had exploded and said she couldn't take being wrapped up in cotton wool. She wanted them all to have a life that was as normal as possible, not live like they were expecting her to die at any second.

'So what was your dad's job?' Maria broke into Emily's thoughts.

Emily smiled, glad to push the earlier not-so-happy recollections away. 'Before Mum got ill, he was head gardener at a stately home. So when they move, with the girls not being around so much and the bungalow being easier to manage, plus Mum being better than we ever hoped she could be, I'm sure he'll find a few part-time gardening jobs on the island.'

'Sure to,' Maria agreed. 'It's often referred to as the Garden Isle, you know.'

'Yes.' Emily nodded. 'It was a lucky day for all of us when Dad saw the bungalow advertised.'

'Lucky for Jarrett as well,' said Maria. 'It's good to see him so happy after — ' Maria broke off as their food arrived.

Emily had ordered *Chiles en nogada* — green chillies stuffed with meat and almonds covered with a walnut sauce with pomegranate kernels sprinkled over. The friendly waitress told her it was also called the 'Independence Dish' because its colours were the same as those of the Mexican flag.

Maria's choice was *Enfrijoladas* — lightly fried tortillas folded and smothered in a sauce made with beans and a selection of delicious toppings. They divided the food between them and, for a while, there was a lull in the conversation while they gave their food the attention it deserved.

Then Emily looked across the table at Maria. 'Lucky for Jarrett after what, Maria?' she asked.

2

'I don't think Jarrett had a particularly good childhood,' Maria said thoughtfully. 'His parents weren't around much and I don't think he got on that well with his brothers. Oh, I don't mean they were always at loggerheads or anything. It was just Jarrett didn't seem to fit in; he liked completely different things. He was always close to his great-uncle and always spent the school holidays at the Manor House.

'Nobody was surprised when Jarrett wanted to go and live there permanently instead of staying in the family home with William and Desmond when their parents died. And of course, even then, Mrs Benson thought the world of Jarrett.'

'You mean Mrs Benson who's Jarrett's housekeeper now?'

Maria nodded. 'She was JP's housekeeper back then. I don't call him

Uncle or Great-unc, like my cousins do,' she added, 'because he isn't really my relation.'

'So how did Mrs Benson end up as Jarrett's housekeeper?'

'She stayed on when JP decided the Manor House was too much responsibility for him and Jarrett bought it,' said Maria. 'I've a feeling William would have liked to buy it but he probably couldn't raise enough money. Besides, it was Jarrett's home, so it was only fair he got first refusal.'

Emily sighed. She was realising more and more how little she knew about Jarrett's life. But maybe that was understandable; when they were together they spent time discussing the future rather than the past.

'Jarrett doesn't talk about his brothers much,' Emily said as she pushed her plate to one side. 'I've met William briefly, but I haven't met Desmond and his wife yet.'

'William's all right but he's the sort who wants to be someone, make an

21

impression,' said Maria. 'I think Hope, his fiancée, is making quite a name for herself. She makes documentary films for television and interviews people with unusual jobs or outlandish hobbies. They'd planned on getting married at the same time as Desmond and Jayne, then something too good to turn down came up and Hope postponed the wedding. Now it's set for August like yours and Jarrett's; that's after Hope's been to Canada to make another documentary. Not sure what it is, exactly. William likes to be mysterious.'

'What about Desmond? What's he like?' Emily asked.

'Desmond is nice. You'll think so too when you've met him,' Maria stated positively. 'And Jayne, his wife, is lovely. They live fairly near Jarrett so I expect you'll see quite a bit of them after you're married. Unless you'll be too busy doing up the house.'

'Doing up the house? Has Jarrett said he wants to?' Emily frowned. She'd only managed a couple of visits but she already loved every nook and cranny of the Georgian manor house in Ponderwell Bay and the acres of rambling gardens, too.

'I take it you don't want to?' said Maria.

'I can't think of anything at all that needs changing or doing up,' said Emily. 'It's perfect as it is.'

Maria gave a dramatic sigh. 'Thank heavens for that. Jarrett's no doubt told you he was engaged to someone very briefly last year.' Jarrett hadn't mentioned it but Emily made a non-committal noise and waited for Maria to continue. 'Well Zelda, who in my opinion was completely wrong for Jarrett in all ways, had big ideas for the house,' Maria explained.

'Big ideas? How?' Emily asked.

'Zelda said it was too staid and too relaxing. She said she wanted visitors to walk in and find something totally different from what they were expecting. She wanted to knock down a few walls and have the downstairs open-plan like . . . '

Maria made inverted commas with her fingers and put on a bored drawling voice, ' . . . like 'those fantastic lofts in converted mills'.'

'It would spoil the whole atmosphere if it was turned into some sort of futuristic home,' Emily said in horror. 'I can't believe Jarrett would have wanted anything like that.'

'He didn't,' Maria said. 'I think that was part of the reason they broke up, though it was just one of the many things they had different views on. She had plans for the gardens, too,' Maria continued. 'Said they needed modern landscaping and wanted to get rid of most of the trees and bushes.'

'That would have been vandalism,' said Emily. 'But come to think of it, there is one thing that will need to be done,' she added thoughtfully. 'We'll need to think of having a rustic fence around the lake. Water and children don't mix.'

'So have you a lot of young relations who'll be visiting?' Maria asked.

Emily shook her head. 'Jarrett and I both want a large family and we plan to start on it straight away.' Maria smiled and Emily felt as though she'd passed some kind of test. 'I mean after we're married of course,' Emily added, aware that her cheeks had turned pink.

The waitress arrived to clear away their empty plates and Emily agreed readily to Maria's suggestion of finishing off with just an ice-cream and a Mexican coffee. 'I expect you're thinking it isn't any of my business even if you did want to make changes to the house and gardens,' said Maria. 'It's just that I'm really fond of Jarrett. He's been good to me and I want to see him settled with someone who'll make him happy. I'm not meaning you're oldfashioned,' she added with a grin, 'but someone with uber-modern ideas about things just wouldn't be right for him.'

Emily nodded. 'From the way he talks about Nursery World products, it's obvious he likes the more traditional things. I'm really looking forward to getting to know more about the business and to meeting his great-uncle. I do hope he's going to be all right.'

'JP's a good age,' said Maria. 'And, even though he's way past his three score years and ten and on extra time, Jarrett will take it hard when that time's up. But I reckon JP should have a few years yet if he agrees to take things a bit easier. He might do when he sees you're interested in Nursery World.'

'Do you think so?' Emily asked. 'I wondered if he might resent a new-comer to the family wanting to know more about things.'

'I'm sure he'll be delighted to tell you all about it,' said Maria. 'He's got quite a thing about wanting it to continue as a family-run business so he'll be thrilled if you tell him you're planning on having a few children.'

Emily laughed. 'I don't know about a few, Maria. When I said a large family, I meant large by today's standards. We're not intending to have enough for a football team. Though Jarrett would probably enjoy coming up with ideas for a footie strip. Actually that's quite an idea, you know. I wonder if Nursery World has a line of sporty clothes for little ones?'

Maria almost choked on her ice-cream. 'Sorry,' she said, chuckling, 'I just had a vision of you and Jarrett looking at a new-born baby and wondering what sort of sporty outfit would suit it best. Seriously, though, it's nice for Jarrett that he can talk to you about his work. I know from experience that being with someone who isn't interested in their partner's work can make things hard.'

They chatted about things other than family and relationships then and, by the time they parted, Emily knew she'd made a new friend. She'd learned a little more about the man she loved, too.

Later, as she settled down for the night, Emily hoped again that Jarrett would be returning the next day; hoped his great-uncle was going to recover; hoped she'd be able to meet the person who meant so much to Jarrett really soon.

* * *

Jarrett phoned on Wednesday morning to tell Emily he'd be with her in the early afternoon.

'Does that mean your great-uncle is going to be all right?' Emily asked.

'For the time being,' Jarrett replied. 'The consultant can't commit himself but he seems to think if Great-unc is careful, takes his medication and avoids any stress or worries, he might be with us a while longer.'

'Well, we'll just have to make sure there isn't anything for him to worry about,' said Emily. She recalled her thoughts of the previous evening — and her mother's view on how to treat someone who was trying to adapt to a different way of life.

'Try to make him take it easy without

wrapping him up in cotton wool too much,' she added. 'Keep other things as normal as possible. Don't stop friends from visiting — just tell them not to stay for too long. Let him feel as if he's still involved in . . . in life. And it might do him good to meet me, you know. Someone new for him to talk to. He must be wondering what I'm like.'

'He knows you're perfect for me. He said as much this morning when we were talking. Which is why . . . ' Jarrett's voice tailed away and Emily thought she heard him sigh.

'Why what, Jarrett?' she prompted.

'It's why I'm going to ask you an enormous favour, Em. I can't talk about it on the phone. We need to be together.' It was clear from Jarrett's voice that he was really worried. Whether it was about the favour, or the anxiety about his great-uncle, Emily didn't know. So she didn't push him to say any more; she just told him she loved him and they'd talk about it later.

* ★ ★

'I know it's a heck of a lot to ask, Em,' Jarrett said. He'd arrived as he'd said he would in the afternoon and, refusing Emily's offer of food or even a drink, had taken twenty minutes to get round to asking the enormous favour.

'But I think,' he continued now, 'Great-unc feels he might not . . . he might not still be with us in August. He sounded so desperate when he said that all he wanted was to be granted enough time to see me happily settled.'

Emily's heart went out to Jarrett. She'd always known he was close to his great-uncle but, since last night when she'd learned more of Jarrett's childhood from Maria, she realised how much of a part his great-uncle had played in that childhood. It was he who'd helped make Jarrett the man he was today. The man she loved; the man she was to spend the rest of her life with.

And if 'the rest of her life' was

destined to begin sooner than she'd expected because Jarrett wanted to bring their wedding forward . . .

'Not only that,' Jarrett added as he paced around her living room. 'I can't help thinking it might give him an extra lease of life. Where are you going?' he asked as Emily jumped up from the chair.

'To phone Neil Anderson. He's the superintendent registrar at the local register office,' she said. 'He's also a family friend so, if he isn't there, I've got his mobile number.'

'You mean . . . Does that mean . . . ?'

Emily ran over to Jarrett and put her arms round him. 'Yes, it means I'll marry you as soon as possible instead of waiting 'til August,' she said.

'Are you sure?' Jarrett asked. 'Are you really sure, Emily?'

'Positive,' she assured him, smoothing away the worry lines on his forehead with her index finger. 'Now,' she said slightly breathlessly, after her assurances had concluded with a long and loving kiss, 'you go and make us a drink while I phone Neil.'

*   *   *

Lynne and Veronica were amazed when Emily told them her news the next day.

'Ten o'clock on the 26th of *this* month, did you say, Em?' Veronica gasped. 'But how can it be so quick, Em?'

'It's just enough days to display the notice on the boards and, luckily, the superintendent registrar is available then,' Emily replied. 'It's a good thing Thursdays are usually quiet; we'll have to close the shop for the morning so you'll both be able to come.'

'But will you find a wedding dress in time? And what will your parents say? And what about your job here?' babbled Veronica. 'You've always said you'd be leaving when you got married, but that was when it was to be August.'

Emily leant back against the shop counter and did a countdown of answers.

'Number one, finding a dress in time will probably be the biggest problem. Two, Jarrett and I went round to see my parents last night. After I'd reassured there'd be no patter of tiny feet in six or seven months — and don't tell me you weren't wondering about that, too . . . ' Emily smiled as she glanced at first one, then the other. ' . . . Anyway, once I'd told them that, they understood that our reason for bringing the wedding forward is for Jarrett's great-uncle's sake.

'My sisters, of course, went crazy with delight. All four of them, because we phoned Carrie in Spain. She won't be able to make it for the wedding, though, but she'll be there in spirit. And as for your third question, Veronica . . . ' Emily looked meaningfully at Lynne.

Lynne nodded and turned to Veronica. 'You're the obvious choice to take over from Emily, Veronica.'

'And if you want to move into the flat once I've cleared all my things?' Emily asked, laughing because she knew

Veronica had been looking for a flat for months.

'Right now though, Veronica,' Lynne said, 'you can start off by coming in the prep room with me to discuss flowers for Emily's wedding. Em, you're relieved as of now. You must have a hundred and one things to do.'

'The most important is finding yourself a gorgeous wedding dress, Emily,' said Veronica. 'You'll probably need to go up to London.'

Emily's mobile rang at that point and Lynne and Veronica made their way to the prep room.

After she'd finished a brief conversation, Emily dashed after them. 'That was Maria. Jarrett's cousin,' she added for Lynne's benefit. 'Veronica can tell you about her after. The important thing is, on the train on his way to London, Jarrett phoned Maria to tell her our news and invite her to the wedding. And, by huge coincidence, Maria has a brand-new and 'out of this world' wedding dress at her place. It's for a big theatrical production next month and Maria is almost sure it will fit me perfectly.'

'So that's your flowers and your dress sorted.' Lynne looked thoughtful. 'What about your reception?'

'We'll need somewhere with wheel-chair access for Mum,' said Emily. 'Maybe I can book a nice restaurant from eleven 'til twelve-thirty. Ask them to put on a wedding brunch. It will have to be something like that. There won't be many guests, just close family and friends. And at such short notice, Jarrett isn't sure his closest friends will be able to come. One's a doctor and one's a solicitor. I expect Mrs Benson will come. She's Jarrett's housekeeper but she's more like family really. So I think there'll only be around sixteen people, and that's including me and Jarrett.'

'You go and try on that dress, Em,' said Lynne, 'then come back here. By then I might have managed to find somewhere for your reception. That's if you'll trust me to do that?'

Emily's reply was a big hug. Then she left to go and see Maria — and the dress she hoped would be 'out of this world' and would fit her.

★ ★ ★

'I feel how Cinderella must have felt when her fairy godmother turned her rags into a ball gown,' Emily said as she stared in delight at her reflection in the mirror.

Maria smiled. 'I knew it would look good.' She reached for a box of pins. 'It will look even better with the sleeves set so,' she added, getting busy with the pins. 'I'll get my needlewoman to do the necessary and bring it to your place on Sunday evening. Will Jarrett be there?'

Emily shook her head. 'I'm seeing him tonight and maybe tomorrow. Then he'll go home until the wedding and spend time doing a few jobs around the house, working, and of course visiting great-uncle. He hasn't decided yet whether to tell him we're getting married earlier than planned. We might just go and see him together on the day after the wedding and take the wedding photos with us.'

'So you aren't going away on honeymoon?' Maria asked as she helped Emily out of the dress.

'Well.' Emily smiled. 'You could say we're honeymooning on the Isle of Wight. Jarrett's going to take time off and we'll go for days out.'

'Not exactly traditional,' said Maria. 'But, seeing as Jarrett won't be with you on Sunday evening when I deliver your dress, you could always invite a couple of friends and your sisters round and we'll have the traditional hen party.'

'As long as you don't make me dress up and walk through the streets wearing a silly hat and stuff, that's a great idea,' said Emily. 'I'll invite Lynne and Veronica so it can double as my leaving party as well.'

After firming up on a few more things, Emily said goodbye to Maria and made her way back to Flower-bunch.

Lynne and Veronica were delighted to hear about the wedding dress and to be invited to the Sunday evening party, and Emily was more than delighted when Lynne told her she'd managed to book a room for the reception at one of the hotels they supplied with flowers every week. 'And they'll find you a bedroom to use for when you change into your going-away outfit,' Lynne added.

'That,' Emily sighed with relief, 'leaves me free to concentrate on other things. Like finding accessories that'll match my beautiful dress.'

So the next days passed mainly in shopping sprees. Her mother and sisters wanted special outfits, too; their mum was easy to please but Clair, Abigail and Sara insisted on looking in every shop before they finally made up their minds. And of course, they wanted something new to wear for Emily's hen party, too.

Before Jarrett arrived on Saturday evening, Emily packed some of her clothes so he could take them back with him. And when he arrived, he told her he was taking her for a quiet, romantic Valentine's Day meal. Naturally enough, their conversation was mainly about their wedding. As he'd thought, his closest friends wouldn't be able to come over for the ceremony, but Desmond and Jayne and probably William and Hope were coming.

'William's in Scotland visiting some of our suppliers,' he said. 'He'll be back by the end of next week, which is good. It means he'll have time to dig out a best man's outfit and he can visit Great-unc, and that will free me up a bit. Mrs Benson's coming,' he added. 'She said she wouldn't miss it for the world. She's decided to take a few days off to give us the house to ourselves. So after the wedding, she'll be going to her sister's in the Cotswolds.'

'So now it will be almost two weeks before I see you again,' Emily sighed after saying goodbye to Jarrett much later that evening.

'We'll talk on the phone every day, Em, love, and I'll be over a couple of days before our wedding.'

3

The following days seemed to fly past. Jarrett arrived early on the day before the wedding but after a quick hello said he'd got shopping to do, and added he'd come straight from his hotel to Emily's parents in the evening for the family meal her mother was putting on. 'Then it will be back to the hotel for me for my last night as a single man,' he said, smiling.

At ten past ten the following morning, wearing the fairytale soft cashmere dress over flimsy silk undies, sheer silk stockings and bronzed high-heeled ankle-tie sandals, and carrying a delicate posy of pink and cream rosebuds, Emily found herself repeating Neil Anderson's words: 'I do solemnly declare that I know not of any lawful impediment why I, Emily Kingston, may not be joined in matrimony to Jarrett Jonathan Gordon.'

They joined hands; the rest was a blur, though she did look down in surprise at the gold band on her finger before realising Jarrett must have bought it yesterday.

Cameras flashed as they signed the register; their signatures were witnessed by Maria and her husband. Then Jarrett led her over to her parents and her younger sisters.

Reaching for Emily's hand, he smiled down at her mother. 'I hope you've forgiven us for not having a church wedding as we'd planned?'

'I think it's really romantic,' said Clair. 'And it was a beautiful ceremony. I never realised before that a register-office wedding could be so . . . so . . . ' She waved her hands around, unable to find the words she wanted. 'I never realised there'd be flowers everywhere.'

'Did you arrange the flowers, Emily?' asked Abigail. 'I remember you telling me once how, if Flowerbunch was supplying the flowers for a register-office wedding, you always tried to do that.'

Emily shook her head and smiled. 'You don't think Veronica and Lynne would have allowed me to arrange my own flowers, do you? That might have brought bad luck.'

'We'd better go and have the rest of the photos taken now, Emily,' said Jarrett. 'Then we can go to the hotel. They've got another reception booked in after ours, remember.'

'I hope it won't take long,' said Sara. 'I'm starving. I was too excited to eat breakfast.'

Emily had always disliked posing for photographs. The photographer implored her to smile but her mouth felt stiff — frozen as if she'd had an injection at the dentist's. *What a way to feel when you've just got married!* That ridiculous analogy made her smile, though, and then her sisters' antics with confetti, bubbles and helium balloons had her laughing.

'That's better,' Jarrett approved. 'We'll need some nice photos for Great-unc. He seemed so much better when I saw him on Monday evening. Kept telling me life must be treating me well because I had a twinkle in my eye. It took me all my time not to tell him we were getting married today.' He lowered his head and brushed Emily's lips with his.

The cameras flashed again. At last the photo session was over and Jarrett guided her to the car waiting to drive them to the hotel for the reception.

'I've never thought it a great idea, this reception lark,' said Emily. 'It seems all wrong somehow, the newly married couple having to spend a couple of hours being chatty and sociable when all they want to do is get away and be alone together.'

Jarrett chuckled. 'Don't worry. Nobody will expect us to stay for long. Your ordeal will soon be over. I'm just sorry we aren't going away on honeymoon, but — '

'I'll be just as happy getting to know my new home better,' Emily assured him.

* * *

There weren't many guests at the reception. Apart from Veronica and Lynne and Simon Hinchcliffe, Jarrett's doctor friend, it was just those in the family who'd managed to come at such short notice. William had been Jarrett's best man — though, Emily thought as she glanced his way, he'd seemed rather gloomy during the short ceremony and didn't look as if he was enjoying himself now.

Once all the speeches and toasts were over Desmond's wife, Jayne, made her way over to Emily so, as she said with a smile, they could get to know each other better.

Jayne was a bubbly chatterbox. All Emily had to do was listen and nod her head occasionally.

'You must call round as soon as you can,' Jayne said warmly. 'We live on what the locals call the Lower Road, way below Jarrett, down the steps. I won't tell you how many there are; you can count them for yourself. And when your parents and sisters come to live on Wight, I'll take you and your mother to meet my brother. He's wheelchair-bound, too. Spina bifida,' she added. 'Which is why I decided to have an amniocentesis test.' She rubbed her stomach lovingly. 'Thank heavens Sally-Anne is going to be all right. Desmond and I succumbed to temptation when we were offered the chance of knowing what sex the baby is,' she confided. 'Now I know, I'm glad. Even though it isn't a boy. Desmond doesn't seem to mind that, either.'

Jayne looked round quickly then spoke with a mischievous grin: 'Of course after Great-uncle springing his surprise yesterday morning, William, who'd never showed any interest in my pregnancy — and I'm six months now — actually phoned from the hospital when he was visiting Great-unc to congratulate me and Desmond. He said how delighted he was it's a girl.'

'William did?' Emily queried.

Jayne laughed and nodded. 'Oh, yes. He would have thought it lengthened the odds for him and Hope. William hadn't seen Hope, you see; he went straight to the hospital after travelling back from Scotland. So it wasn't until he got home that he heard from Hope you two were getting married today.' Jayne laughed again. 'I don't know why Great-unc didn't tell him.'

Emily hadn't understood much of Jayne's chatter. But she could reply sensibly to that last sentence. 'He didn't know,' she said. 'Jarrett didn't want to tell him in case — '

'Oh, goodness,' Jayne interrupted with a gasp. 'Great-unc does know. I chatted about your wedding when I visited him on Monday. It was just after Jarrett had been, so of course I thought . . . Oh,' she wailed. 'Jarrett should have told me he was keeping it a secret. I hope he won't be too mad at me.'

'I'll tell him not to be,' Emily said.

Jayne seemed to stop worrying after that because she went on, 'I do wish I'd been there to see William's face when he found out. He sounded furious when he phoned Desmond. Then they both went off to see Great-unc. You know, I suspect William might bring his wedding forward now.'

Jayne's spate of information was whirling round Emily's brain in half-finished sentences that made no sense, like tadpoles swimming against a strong current. She stared into her glass. 'I think I've had too much champagne.'

'Well, why not?' responded Jayne. 'After all, you only get married once. At least, that's the way I feel about it. I believe in 'happy ever after', don't you, Emily?'

'I certainly do believe in it,' said Emily.

'What do you believe in, Emily?' She felt Jarrett's arm around her shoulder and leaned happily against him. 'Never mind,' he said softly, 'you can tell me later. Right now, your sisters are waiting to help you get changed.'

'Don't forget, I'll expect to see you

when you come up for air,' Jayne called as Emily allowed herself to be led away by her sisters.

⋆ ⋆ ⋆

The pale green suit Emily had bought on the shopping trip was laid out on the bed; the cream soft suede shoes she'd been unable to resist were on the floor next to her travelling bag and, to her surprise, there was a matching shoulder bag on the dressing table.

'Jarrett phoned yesterday and asked if we could think of something you'd like as a surprise present,' said Sara. 'We all saw you looking longingly at that gorgeous, very expensive shoulder bag when you bought the shoes, Em, so we told him which shop it was in and what colour to get.'

'But don't stand there dreaming, Emily,' Abigail laughed. 'The quicker you get changed, the quicker your dream will come true. Come here and let me undo your zip. We must be careful not to muss your hair too much.'

'I'll do your hair for you,' offered Clair. 'I'm sure there'll be a comb in here,' she added, giggling as she opened the shoulder bag. 'Oh, what a gorgeous scarf,' she said, putting it on the dressing table. She rootled around inside the bag again. 'And what's this I can feel?' She drew out an oblong jeweller's box and handed it to Emily.

'Oh, wow,' Abigail gasped when Emily opened the box to reveal a delicate gold wristwatch.

Next came a key ring complete with a front and back door key, a soft leather purse, a designer make-up pouch and . . . 'I feel a tiny bottle,' squeaked Clair. 'Is it perfume?'

Emily shook her head. She hadn't the faintest idea what was in the shoulder bag. It wouldn't surprise me too much if a rabbit came out, she thought as she watched her sister pull out an attractively shaped bottle.

Clair opened the bottle and sniffed. 'It's fantastic,' she said happily. 'A lovely soft, flowery smell. Isn't it romantic how Jarrett chose such gorgeous things?'

'Nothing could be more romantic than the way he looked at Emily when they said their wedding vows,' Sara said with a happy sigh. 'You know,' she added, 'right from the day we met him, the three of us always wished your wedding wasn't planned for such a long way ahead.'

'We're moving into the bungalow next month,' said Clair. 'So we'll all come to you and Jarrett for an Easter party. And then after Easter we'll — '

'After Easter we'll be going to boarding school,' chorused Sara and Abigail.

'And Mum will be much better because she won't have so much work to do when we're not there,' said Clair. 'She can spend a lot of time in the garden, knitting, sewing, maybe painting. Dad calls it the Garden Isle; he says you don't get cold weather on the island.'

'It's all just like a fairytale come true

for all of us,' said Sara as she held out a cream shoe for Emily to slip her foot into. 'See, the slipper fits, Cinderella, and Jarrett's the handsome prince who found his true love. And — '

'You look really beautiful, Em,' Abigail interrupted Sara, moving swiftly to the fitted wardrobe. 'Now all you need is the finishing touch. Voila,' she said, reaching inside the wardrobe and bringing out a cashmere coat. 'We hid it away earlier,' she added.

'It's from us three and Carrie and Mum and Dad,' said Clair as Abigail buttoned Emily into it. 'And here's your posy, Em. You'll have to throw it but I've put two rosebuds in your bag so you can press them in your wedding album.'

* * *

When Emily walked down the hotel stairs her heart tilted as she met Jarrett's gaze and she felt her cheeks fill with warmth when he said, 'Well, Emily

Gordon, shall we go?' Something elusive stirred in her mind but, before she could attempt to catch it, Jarrett put his arm around her shoulders and they began to make their way outside to the waiting cab.

Friendly voices and silly jokes followed them and a shower of confetti whirled round. Smiling, Emily threw her posy towards her sisters before Jarrett handed her into the taxi.

Then he was sitting next to her, his arms around her again, his lips seeking and finding hers, to the delight of the waving guests.

But something wasn't right. Jarrett seemed tense; it wasn't a warm and tender kiss, or one filled with desire. More like . . . more like a dutiful kiss, Emily thought as Jarrett moved his mouth from hers and leaned back in the seat.

'What's wrong, Jarrett?' she asked quietly. 'Is something wrong? You haven't had bad news about your great-uncle, have you?'

'No.' He shook his head. 'I think I'm just a bit dazed.'

'It does feel strange knowing we're now man and wife,' she agreed.

He nodded and reached for her hand. And the rest of the short journey was made in silence.

When they got out of the taxi, Jarrett paid the fare and picked up her travelling bag. Then they made their way towards the catamaran. Emily knew the journey across the Solent would only take around half an hour, yet she suddenly felt as if she was leaving everything she knew and going to a faraway land.

As if guessing her thoughts, Jarrett took her arm and said, 'It won't be long before your parents and sisters move into the bungalow, and in the meantime we can set up video calls.' He'd sounded cool and distracted; Emily wondered if the thought of her missing her family hurt him.

He guided her to a seat, stowed her travelling bags underneath it, then sat down beside her. The minutes ticked by; a group of laughing, chattering passengers found themselves seats. Emily moved closer to Jarrett. She tried telling herself she was imagining his tenseness, his unresponsiveness. But it didn't work.

★ ★ ★

Jarrett's thoughts were tearing at his insides. There *was* something wrong and he couldn't stop dwelling on the problem; it filled his mind, destroying his earlier happiness. He still found what he'd been told while Emily was getting changed hard to believe.

At first he'd thought it was William's idea of a joke. Then seeing his brother's anger, he'd dismissed that idea and suggested that William had misunderstood what their great-uncle had said. But when Desmond joined them, he'd confirmed everything William said. A phone call to the hospital when, after a lot of persuasion, he'd been allowed to speak to Great-unc had left no doubt in his mind; it was all awfully, terribly true.

What I don't understand, Jarrett thought now, *is why, when he'd no idea I was marrying Emily today, did Great-unc suddenly decide to tell William and Desmond what he'd done? And why did he order William to tell me? Not that William believed I needed to be told. He . . .*

'We're moving. We're on our way.' Emily's lacklustre statement broke into his thoughts. He turned his head to look at her. She was huddled into her cream coat, staring straight ahead, and he wondered if she knew she'd spoken the words aloud. The almost visible shadow of loneliness and bewilderment surrounding her reached out and clutched at his guts. It wasn't meant to be like this.

He felt bile rise at the back of his throat as his stomach churned with anxiety and despair. How could he expect Emily to believe that until today he'd had no idea of what his great-uncle had done if William, his own brother, didn't believe it? Maybe it would be best not to mention it to Emily. But was keeping such a thing from the woman he loved with his heart and soul any way to start married life?

4

'I booked a car and driver,' Jarrett said as they made their way off the catamaran and towards the pier gates. 'I didn't want to spend time fetching my own car from the car park.' Emily nodded and shivered. Jarrett obviously noticed her shivering because he put his arm around her, pulling her close. 'Cold or nervous?' he asked.

She looked up at him and when she saw the tenderness written on his face, her earlier worries and feeling of loneliness began to fade. 'Bit of both, I think,' she replied.

Jarrett nodded. 'All that will change when we get home,' he said, dropping a light kiss on her forehead. 'And that will be very soon, sweetheart, because here's our car.'

'I've got the car heater going,' the driver greeted them. 'It's unusually cold.'

He shook his head. 'We don't often have real winter weather here and I've certainly never known it in February.'

The car was warm, the back seat comfortable and luxurious; Emily leaned back with a sigh of relief. Everything was going to be all right after all. It was only a short journey. When Emily got out of the car she watched Jarrett pick up her travelling bags; then he put his arm around her, guiding her up the steps to the front door. Icy rain fell hard and sharp on her face. She took a deep breath and an elusive scent from the flowerbeds below filled her nostrils. She tried to name the fragrance as Jarrett put her bags down and inserted his key in the lock.

It's like fairground candyfloss, she thought, and knew she'd remember the smell for the rest of her life because at that very moment Jarrett, after grabbing her bags and placing them inside, swept her into his arms and carried her over the threshold, kicking the door shut behind them.

'Home,' he said. His voice was husky and Emily wished she could see his face properly; he'd sounded glad but also uncertain. *Or maybe, like me, he's a bit nervous about our first night of married life together,* she thought as he put her down and flicked on the hall lights. Perhaps that was why he'd been so quiet, so distant during their journey over.

As Jarrett slipped off her coat and his own, throwing them on a nearby chair, Emily glanced around and a feeling of peace descended over her. The walls were panelled and their patina glowed warmly, enhancing the silk hangings and the softly muted rugs on the hall floor. The staircase was wide and carved with barley-sugar balusters: light oak, like the beautifully polished doors which led to the downstairs rooms.

Jarrett opened the sitting room door and Emily obeyed his unspoken invitation to enter. 'The heating's on,' he said, 'but I'll go and turn it up, then I'll put a match to the fire.' He gestured to the ready-laid fire in the grate beneath the gilded pinewood mantelpiece. 'You could close the curtains and pour us a drink while I'm gone,' he added from the doorway. 'We'll soon be warm and comfortable.'

*   *   *

Jarrett opened his eyes and wondered why his shoulder hurt before realising the pins and needles came from the weight of Emily's head. It felt good to have it resting there — to have her sleeping like a baby in his arms. He'd obviously fallen asleep, too, after they'd drunk a small glass of brandy in between long, lingering kisses.

Thank heavens he'd managed to come to a decision before they'd got off the ferry at Ryde. He went through it again in his mind. Yes, he was still sure he'd be able to talk his great-uncle round. Make him see how much harm it would do, what misery and doubt it would cause, and get the old boy to undo what he'd done. And Emily would never know about it.

He eased himself away from her and gently manoeuvred her body into a comfortable position. Straightening up, he stretched and yawned, then smiled as Emily made a strange little noise in her sleep. Maybe she was missing the warmth of his body.

After covering her with a rug from the back of the sofa he moved quietly over to the fireplace. He hadn't got round to lighting the fire earlier. Emily had looked so adorable when he'd come into the room after turning up the heating that holding her, loving her, had been the only thing on his mind.

He added an extra fire-lighter to the ready-laid fire before putting a match to it, then nodded with satisfaction as it caught quickly, the flames eagerly lighting the small pyramid of sticks and fuel.

Maybe it was the crackling noise that woke Emily. She made another small noise in her throat then, as he had done, she stretched and yawned.

Smiling, he rose from the hearthrug and went back to the sofa. He bent over her, examining her face in the soft glow cast from the table lamps, then traced a line on her cheeks.

'You smell of fire-lighters,' she murmured, as his fingers wandered across the top of her mouth. He laughed and ruffled her hair and laughed again as he watched her struggling to raise herself into a sitting position. 'I feel all floaty and light-headed,' she said. 'It must be the brandy I drank.'

'Nope, it can't be the brandy. You only had a few drops. More likely it was this.' He bent over her and kissed her. 'Or,' he said a few minutes later, 'maybe it's hunger. Food is what you need, sweetheart. You can't have eaten much all day. You rest a while longer and after I've brought in some logs, I'll go and rustle something up.'

'I know you're good at making sandwiches and toast,' she said. 'But can you cook?'

He could, though he had been intending to get something Mrs Benson had cooked out of the freezer. Suddenly, though, he wanted to prepare and cook a meal for her. 'You'll have to wait and see,' he teased.

★   ★   ★

Emily felt deliciously content and a warm glow flowed through her as she watched Jarrett walk towards the sitting room door. She hadn't realised before but he must have changed his clothes when he'd gone to turn up the heating.

He was wearing petrol-blue cords which fitted his slim hips and leather-belted waist like a second skin. The rust-coloured roll-neck sweater emphasised his long back and broad shoulders. His thick black hair had sprung into slightly unruly waves, and her fingertips tingled.

Then he was gone, but his presence still lingered in the room. She nestled down again amongst the brightly coloured cushions, watched the flames flickering up the chimney, and dreamed happy dreams of the future.

When Jarrett returned he brought with him a cold blast of air from outside and a basket of logs. He crouched to put a log on the fire. She heard a small sizzle as its dampness met the heat, breathed in the pungent aroma and watched a grey wispiness swirling lazily.

'Wrap the rug around you and come with me,' said Jarrett, placing the guard in front of the fire.

Her legs and arms obeyed with lazy reluctance. She followed him into the kitchen and over to the open back door.

'Isn't it beautiful?' he whispered, as though by speaking normally he might spoil the effect — the effect of the hundreds of tiny snowflakes dancing merrily, caught in the beams of the outside lights, dancing over the flowering shrubs and bushes which seemed to edge their way into the kitchen. 'It hardly ever snows here,' he said, still whispering, 'and certainly not in February.'

'It's like something out of a fairy tale,' she whispered back. And as she stood close to him in the open doorway, the scene imprinted itself firmly in her heart, to be locked away with the memory of the scent of candyfloss. 'What is it that smells like candyfloss?' she asked, realising she could smell it here, too.

'Hemerocallis, also known as Sweet Sugar Candy.' He pointed to some clumps of plants with strap-like leaves and large pink flowers with ruffled edges.

'I wish we could walk round the garden,' she said on a sigh.

'We can do whatever we like,' he teased, eyes darkening as he looked down into her face.

'I've no proper shoes.' She held up a foot. 'I didn't pack boots. They're still at the flat with all the other stuff to bring over. I didn't think I'd need them here at this time of year. I was expecting it to be spring-type weather.'

'Didn't you look to see what was in your travelling bags?' he asked. She shook her head and he smiled. 'Wait here,' he told her.

She took a step outside and leant against the wall. Childishly, she stuck out her tongue and chuckled happily when a snowflake landed and melted with delicious iciness inside her warm mouth.

'You will go to the ball, Cinderella.' Emily turned then and gasped in delight. Jarrett was holding a pair of honey-brown cords, a matching mohair sweater and a pair of comfortable-looking ankle boots of the softest leather.

'I knew you didn't have time to pack all your clothes,' he said. 'So I bought you an outfit suitable for exploring the island. I didn't know at the time you'd be needing it on our wedding night, though.' He smiled again, pulled her inside and closed the door.

'I'll go and change in front of the fire,' she said and, taking the clothes from him, she hurried away to the sitting room.

The textures pleased her as she

smoothed them down over her rounded curves. Walking over to the mirror, she was amazed how Jarrett had guessed her size so accurately.

'You look like a friendly pixie in that outfit,' Jarrett said from the doorway. Emily turned to see him holding out her boots. 'It's a shame these haven't got pointed toes,' he added. 'Sit down and I'll put them on for you.' The warmth and tenderness in his voice made her legs tremble. She sank quickly onto the winged chair with its unusual scrolled ears, and watched him walking towards her.

His hands lingered far longer than necessary as he pushed her feet into the boots and she was sure his fingers trembled when he tied the laces. His hand seemed steady enough, though, when it took hers in a firm clasp to pull her out of the chair. 'Now for our coats,' he said.

They walked into the hall where he reached her coat from the chair and placed it around her shoulders. He opened a carved oak hall cupboard and passed her a woollen scarf before taking his sheepskin jacket from its hanger. She watched as he donned the sheepskin, admiring the way his chest expanded as he pushed his arms into the sleeves, and wondered if she really wanted to spend time in the garden instead of . . .

'Well?' he said, 'are we going to explore the winter wonderland, or are we going to stand in the hall admiring each other?'

So he knew what her thoughts had been, did he? She felt the colour rising in her cheeks and moved quickly ahead of him into the kitchen. She opened the back door with a flourish and hurried outside, laughing as she made a footprint in the light sprinkling of snow which had settled on the ground. The falling flakes weren't as tiny now.

'You're beginning to look like a snowman,' Jarrett laughed. 'Here, you take the torch.' He put an arm around her shoulders, drawing her body close to his side as they started to walk slowly down the path.

She could hear the slightly muffled sound of their feet in the stillness and another noise she couldn't quite place. A gentle rustling and a soft clinking. Metal on metal?

She stopped. Jarrett stopped, too. So did the noise. Just as she noticed Jarrett was carrying something, he turned to face her. 'Why have we stopped?'

'I couldn't work out what the strange noise was,' she explained, pointing to the carrier bag dangling from his fingers. 'Whatever have you got in there?'

'Wait and see,' he replied mysteriously, dropping his arm from her shoulder and reaching for her hand.

They wandered down the stone steps between the magnificent rock gardens and now she could hear the miniature waterfalls flowing lazily and sleepily. 'It truly is a winter wonderland,' Emily sighed in delight and shone the torch in the direction of one of the waterfalls. 'Look, I'm making snowbeams.' She'd never seen such beauty before; she smiled as the snowflakes danced on the blue shadows, the torch's rays turning them to muted pinks and yellows, the colours reflected in the tumbling water.

'I'm sure snowbeams must have the power to make wishes come true,' said Jarrett. 'What shall we wish for, Emily? I think we should wish for warmth and food.'

'No, don't let's go in yet,' she protested. 'I want to stay out here. Let's go . . . ' She darted away from him, closed her eyes and twirled around. Then she pointed the torch and opened her eyes. 'Let's go over there.'

He chuckled and said, 'I didn't know I'd given you a magic torch. It knows exactly where I want to take you to grant our wish.' His voice was husky and Emily gazed sideways under her eyelashes at him, but he was looking straight ahead and she couldn't see his eyes.

He led her past a weeping willow tree and now she noticed a summerhouse standing proudly at the top of a snow-covered knoll. 'It will be cosy inside, even on a night like this,' Jarrett told her. Opening the door, he continued, 'When he was younger, Great-unc often used to spend the night here watching for badgers, so he furnished it simply but comfortably and had heating and electricity put in.'

He flicked a switch and Emily gave a gasp surprise and pleasure. There were bright rugs on the polished wooden floor, a squashy studio couch, and a wicker basket-chair sat temptingly near a black metal stove.

'The stove burns logs,' Jarrett said. 'But it takes ages for it to warm the place up so it isn't worth lighting it now. We'll have to make do with quick and easy.' He walked over to the wooden table which was close to one of the large windows, put the carrier bag down, then reached under the table to pull out a small electric fire.

Emily laughed. 'You know, this — ' She waved her hands around. ' — is like a picture I once saw of a play house built for a child princess. There's even a cooker.'

'And I'll switch the cooker on,' he said. 'Ages ago, I promised to make you something to eat. But you saw the snow and wanted to play out. However . . . ' Smiling, he stepped over to the table and reached into the carrier bag.

'You're crazy.' She giggled as he produced eggs, a carton of cream, bunches of dried herbs, a slab of butter, a crusty loaf, a frying pan, a bowl, a fish slice, knives and forks, plates, two glasses wrapped in a linen tea towel, a bottle of wine, and a corkscrew.

'I can't take any credit for the unusual weather.' He picked a lingering snow-flake from his sleeve and put it on the palm of his hand. As they watched it melting he added, 'But I hope this first meal alone together as man and wife will stay in your mind and in your heart forever.' He took off his sheepskin jacket and hung it over the back of the wicker chair, then smiled at her before reaching for the frying pan and the butter.

She watched him beating the eggs, adding cream and a sprinkling of herbs, and before long a tempting smell filled the air.

'Take your coat off; it's warm in here now and you'll feel more comfortable without it while you're eating,' he said. 'The omelettes are almost ready.'

Jarrett poured the wine, served the delectable golden omelettes, then lit two candles he'd found in a cupboard and dimmed the lights, leaving an outside spotlight shining onto the lake below them. The table was small and intimate; they sat side by side on the wooden bench, thighs almost touching. The snow-flakes still flurried outside; there were so many windows in the summerhouse, Emily felt as though the two of them were fairy-tale figures imprisoned happily inside a snow-scene paperweight.

'Hang on,' he said. 'I've forgotten some-thing.' He got up, went over to his sheepskin jacket and reached into one of the deep pockets. 'Flowers and music,' he said, walking back and handing her a single yellow rose before switching on the CD player he'd brought with him.

Emily touched the delicate petals of the rose as the sweet, soft strains of a Brahms symphony tiptoed through the summerhouse and into her heart, filling it with yet another memory to cherish.

'Hey, dreamer, don't let your omelette go cold.' Smiling, Jarrett picked up her knife and fork and cut a small piece of the omelette. 'Open your mouth.'

As she savoured the tasty morsel, he removed the rose from her fingers and, sitting down, laid it next to her plate. Then he handed her his fork. 'You can feed me now.' His deep navy gaze captured hers and, enslaved, she obeyed him.

They'd shared meals before but it had never been like this. Her hand trembled as the fork moved closer to his mouth, his partly open lips, his strong white teeth, the tip of his tongue. His hand came over hers, guiding it closer, his tongue feathering across her finger-tips before curling over the fork to take the food into his mouth.

Oh, heavens. Watching him chew and swallow; the way his cheeks, his mouth, his chin moved . . . *Breathe, breathe.* She'd got to breathe. The short, shallow breaths echoed in her ears and felt as if they were deafening her.

'My turn now,' he said. The slow, exquisite torture continued as turn by turn they fed each other; turn by turn held the wine glass to each other's lips.

And then their plates and glasses were empty. Emily picked up the yellow rose and breathed in its perfume.

'I'll give you one yellow rose on every special occasion,' Jarrett said. He took her hand, pulled her to her feet and led her to the soft, squashy couch. They sank onto it together. His face came close and her lips parted to accept his, responding to the silent commands of his mouth. His tongue touched hers, turning her bones to fiery liquid. The kiss deepened and she melted against him and pulled him even closer.

5

Next morning Jarrett got up early, prepared a breakfast tray and carried it to the bedroom. He gazed down at Emily as she lay sleeping and smiled when he saw she was holding their rose. He hadn't realised she'd brought it back with her from the summerhouse.

Putting the tray down, he walked over to the window and opened the curtains. He couldn't wait to find out what Emily would say when he told her they were snowed in.

The sudden brightness flooding the room woke Emily. 'What time is it?' she asked.

'Seven-thirty.' Jarrett moved to the small table. 'I've brought you breakfast.'

Emily's toes curled in delight as she remembered the previous evening: eating the meal he prepared for her in the summerhouse; snuggling together on the squashy sofa listening to soft romantic music while outside the snowflakes whirled.

As he poured two mugs of coffee from an insulated jug, Jarrett's lips quirked in a smile as if he knew what she were thinking. The fragrant aroma tempted her, and she needed something mundane to do while she tried to control her thoughts. She reached for a mug as soon as he put the tray on the bed.

He opened up a foil package. 'I wrapped the toast in here to keep it warm,' he said, handing her a slice. He picked up another piece, and his coffee, and went to sit on the cushioned window-seat.

Biting into her toast, Emily watched him from under her eyelashes. He sat sideways-on, one long leg stretched along the seat. He'd pushed up the sleeves of his sweater and she could see a scatter of dark hair on his forearm. Her gaze travelled to his firm wrist, his hand and the long fingers over the slice of toast as he lifted it to his mouth. Her own mouth dried; it was hard to swallow and she almost choked on her toast.

'Something go down the wrong way?' he asked with a wicked smile. Emily felt her cheeks go pink. He must have read her thoughts again. Two seconds later she knew for sure that he had. He came back to the bed; breakfast was forgotten as last night's memories faded and were replaced with new ones.

* * *

'I forgot to tell you,' Jarrett said much later. 'We're snowed in. I hope Desmond and Jayne didn't get stranded anywhere. Or if they did, I hope they found somewhere comfortable to stay. I expect Jayne needs comfort right now.'

Jarrett's words reminded Emily of something Jayne had said at the reception. 'Why should William be delighted Jayne's baby is a girl?' she asked. 'It's nothing to do with him.'

'He probably fancies dangling a niece from his knees,' Jarrett replied after a small silence.

'Jayne's really thrilled the baby's a girl and she said Desmond doesn't seem to mind,' Emily continued. 'It was a strange conversation. Why should Desmond mind? He should be thankful the baby's all right. That's why Jayne had tests, isn't it? To make sure she wasn't having a spina bifida baby.'

'Of course Desmond's thankful the baby's going to be all right. It was a terrible time for them, waiting to get all the results.'

'Maybe Desmond thought he wanted a son until he knew the baby was a girl,' said Emily. 'Mum and Dad would have liked a son. I think that's why there are so many of us. But we always felt loved and wanted even though we're all girls.'

'That must be a nice feeling,' said Jarrett. 'I don't think my parents really wanted any of us. Well, maybe William was planned, but Desmond and I certainly weren't.'

Briefly, Emily glimpsed the tormented shadows in Jarrett's eyes and her heart went out to him. He seemed to have withdrawn into himself as though he regretted telling her about his parents. His face looked tight and closed now, his body tense; he was obviously lost in those shadows of the past.

I'll make it up to you, she vowed silently. *I'll give you all the love you never had.* 'I'm getting up,' she said, throwing off the quilt and shifting towards the edge of the bed. 'We'll act like kids and go and build a snowman.'

Jarrett laughed. 'I think we'd best clear a path to the wood shed first.'

Jarrett found her a donkey jacket and a pair of Mrs Benson's wellies. Together, they dug a path to the wood shed and made several laughter-filled journeys there and back to the house armed with logs. 'I haven't been thinking straight,' said Jarrett, shaking his head. 'There's a sledge in the cellar. I should have got it out and we could have piled the logs onto it.'

'Huh. Now you tell me. I know what you could get, though. Have you got a magnifying glass?'

'Yes, what do you want it for?'

Emily chuckled. 'Go and get it and I'll show you.'

'Yes, ma'am.' He grinned at her and tugged his forelock before disappearing into the house.

Emily let out her breath in a contented sigh. The weather was giving her a great chance to show Jarrett some of the things he might have missed out on as a young boy.

'Your wish is my command.' He'd come up behind her and, reaching over her shoulder, waved a large magnifying glass in front of her face. 'It's Mrs B's. She uses it for reading recipes in a hand-written book which has been in her family for years.'

She reached up and took it from him. Then, stepping sideways, she held it over the snowflakes on the sleeve of her navy jacket. 'Look at the patterns,' she said.

Their heads close, they examined the six-pointed pattern of each flake. 'No two are ever the same,' she marvelled. 'When I was little, I used to try and draw the patterns, but the snowflakes always melted away too soon.'

'I love hearing about things you did when you were little,' he said.

'In that case, we'll build that snowman now and I'll tell you more.'

Emily chatted as they worked. 'I remember one year when it snowed at Easter. Mum and Dad crept outside on the Saturday night and built a snowman. They hid presents in it — tiny little eggs, fluffy yellow chicks, an Easter bunny and packets of flower seeds. Sweet peas and marigolds I think. Best of all, I found a little silver heart with a snowflake design engraved on it. The strange thing is, Mum and Dad still to this day deny putting the heart there.'

'Have you still got it?' Jarrett asked.

Emily nodded. 'It's in my memento box at the flat. I'm a terrible hoarder,' she confessed. 'I can't bear to throw things away.'

'We'll have to bring all your belongings over soon,' he said, running a finger down her cheek and smiling into her eyes. 'They'll make you feel more at home.'

'What I feel right now is hungry,' she told him. 'Let's finish the snowman later and go indoors for toast and coffee. It's a shame the fire isn't lit yet. We could have made fire toast. I love doing that.'

'After we've had a snack we'd better check the food supplies,' Jarrett said. 'Mrs Benson probably thought we'd be eating out while we're still on honeymoon. She certainly won't have allowed for us being snowed in.'

★ ★ ★

Modernity blended happily with original features in the scullery. Emily was fascinated with the old marble cooling slab and the stone sink. Jarrett smiled and led her over to the large deep-freeze and they examined its contents. 'We won't starve,' he said. 'I'm glad there's some steak. I've a weakness for steak pudding.'

'I'm a dab hand at suet and pastry,' Emily told him. 'It's not exactly healthy eating, but shall we be really greedy and have a steak pudding followed by an apple pie? That's if there are any apples.'

He nodded. 'They're stored up in the attics, in the traditional way.'

'Let's go and get some now. I've not seen the attics yet.'

'I'll light the fire in the sitting room first, then it will be nice and warm when we come back down.'

The first thing Emily noticed when they went into the attics was a wooden rocking horse. 'He's beautiful. Why on earth is he hidden away up here where nobody can see him and touch him? Move him out for me, Jarrett. I must have a go on him.'

Whilst she rocked gently back and

forth, Jarrett told her that the rocking horse was the first one his great-uncle had ever made. 'I suppose you could call it the flagship of Nursery World,' he mused. 'We still make our rocking horses to this exact design today. Great-unc takes a special interest in the rocking horses and the baby wear, particularly in boys' clothes.' Jarrett's air of relaxed enthusiasm had been replaced by something Emily couldn't name.

'I must show him the romper-suit I made when Mum was expecting Clair,' she said, striving to dispel the air of unease. 'I thought I'd be sure to get a brother if I made boys' clothes. Of course I didn't, and the romper-suit got tucked away in — '

'In your memento box,' guessed Jarrett. 'You know, there's a trunk here somewhere. Its contents will interest you. Old photos, toys, books, my sand paintings and I can't recall what else.'

'Your sand paintings? Do you mean they belong to you, or that you painted them?'

'Both,' he replied. He reached up to lift her down and she slid into his arms. He held her close and she rested her head on his chest. She could feel his heart beating, a steady comforting beat. She could feel his lips on her hair and she clasped her hands together over his spine, drawing him even closer. It was a beautiful time, a melding of their souls, binding them together in gentle contentment.

He kissed her forehead before releasing her, then touched the place he'd kissed with his fingertip. 'Let's find that trunk,' he suggested, quirking an eyebrow as he looked into her eyes. Her heart somersaulted and, taking the hand he held towards her, she felt like she might explode with happiness.

When Jarrett opened the trunk, Emily knelt down and began taking things out, putting them to one side of her on the floor.

'I thought you'd examine every item as you came to it,' Jarrett said.

'I can't wait to see your sand

paintings; I'll look at everything else afterwards. Ah, this must be them.'

They'd been packed away carefully, each one of them protected by soft plastic bubble wrap.

'You unwrap them,' she said, shuffling along on her knees to make room for him.

There were landscapes, seascapes, delicate portrayals of flowers and birds and a picture of an ivy-covered thatch-roofed inn.

'That's the inn near the one where the poet Longfellow used to stay,' Jarrett told her. 'I love his *Hiawatha*, though he wrote it years before he visited the island. But he did write an inscription for the fountain outside the inn. I'll show it to you one day.'

'I'd like that,' Emily said. 'Jarrett, these are good, really good. Why don't you do some more? Some nursery rhyme scenes with all the characters wearing Nursery World designed clothes?'

'I've got an idea you and Great-unc are going to get on really well together.

He likes anyone who shows a genuine interest in Nursery World. I just can't understand — ' He broke off abruptly and Emily wondered why.

But she'd found the photograph albums and was eagerly turning the pages, hoping to find some photos of Jarrett when he was young.

'Why don't we take the albums downstairs?' suggested Jarrett. 'It's not exactly warm up here.'

'You're right, it isn't,' Emily agreed. 'I didn't notice the cold until you mentioned it. I'll take your sand paintings down, too. I want a closer look at them.'

They were halfway downstairs before they realised they hadn't got the apples. Laughing, Jarrett turned and went back to fetch some.

*   *   *

The sitting room fire was blazing merrily, the logs filling the room with the scent of apple. Emily sat in one of the armchairs in front of the fire, the unopened photograph albums on her lap. Jarrett lay on the floor, his head against her knees; and as she watched the snowflakes dancing against the tall windows, she knew she had never felt happier.

Jarrett was asleep when she finally decided to look at the photos again. He hadn't told her anything about his childhood, except for the one hurtful moment when he'd said he and Desmond hadn't been wanted; maybe the photos would tell her more.

But they didn't. There were none of the usual family-type photos most people had. These were mainly of scenery — places Emily didn't recognise, and she wondered if Jarrett's parents had spent their time travelling round the world.

As she got towards the end of the second album, a torn envelope fell out. It was addressed to Mr J. P. Gordon. Jarrett's middle name was Jonathan. The contents of the envelope must have been sent to Great-unc, she mused, and was about to slip the envelope back into the album when a photograph fell out.

Emily looked down at it. For a moment she couldn't believe what she was seeing. She had the very same photograph in her memento box. A photograph of herself, taken on her seventh birthday.

Her birthday party had been cancelled because Carrie had the measles. To make up for the disappointment, her grandparents had taken her out for the day. They'd let her choose the place and she'd chosen one they'd often been to — an isolated country inn with a children's playground. Often, too, they'd met a friend of her grandparents there — a big, friendly man with a grey beard and a gruff voice. Emily had called him Uncle Bear.

Uncle Bear had always had a boy with him. A tall, dark-haired boy with laughing eyes. A boy who, even in his early teens, had been willing to amuse Emily while their elders sat and talked.

The boy who was in the photograph with her. The boy the young Emily had loved with all her heart.

Uncle Bear had disappeared for a while that day, and when he returned he'd called Emily over and handed her a tiny wrapped parcel. 'A present from both of us,' he'd said in his lovely gruff voice. 'A present from me and your boyfriend.'

She could remember leaning against Uncle Bear's knee as she opened her parcel and whispering: 'I'm going to marry him when I grow up.' Could remember her delight when inside the wrapping she'd found an autograph book.

Everyone wrote something in the book. Uncle Bear had said the words out loud as he'd written: 'Emily now, Emily forever, Kingston now but not forever. In years to come, we will see, I wonder what your name will be?'

Then he'd added something in tiny writing at the bottom of the page and folded the corner over. 'It tells you what you'll be called when you're grown up and married,' he'd said.

She'd turned the corner back, to read the name — her own name, followed by one that was easy for a seven-year-old to read. 'Emily Gordon!' she'd declared.

That was the last visit to the country inn with her grandparents. Her grandfather had died a month after her seventh birthday and her grandmother a year later. She'd gone just once again with her parents and Carrie but they'd been the only people there. So she'd never seen Uncle Bear or the boy again, the boy she'd thought of as Gordon, her conception of surnames being vague at that age.

So *that* was the elusive memory that ran through my mind at the wedding reception, Emily thought now. Uncle Bear telling her she'd be called Emily Gordon. 'And now here I am.' She spoke the last words aloud; they fell into the silence, waking Jarrett.

'What did you say?' he asked on a yawn. He stretched, his hands moving up Emily's legs, over her knees and onto her lap, dislodging the photograph albums.

She leant forward, trying to catch them as they slid to the floor. He captured her wrists as her hands came down over his hips and pinioned them to the floor.

Then he lifted his face. It was flushed and warm from the heat of the fire and she could see the faint, dark shadowing on his cheeks and chin.

The logs moved in the grate, sending up tiny sparks and igniting with the invisible sparks surrounding them as their lips finally met. She'd never kissed upside-down before; she found it stimulating and . . . and amusing.

They were still kissing when she chuckled and the echo of her chuckle vibrated in her chest. Jarrett released her wrists and then her lips, and rolled over.

'Come down here with me, Emily,' he said and, smiling, Emily slid into his waiting arms.

Emily woke some time later to feel the feathering of Jarrett's lips on her eyelids; it was an achingly sweet caress — a caress of a shared wonderful time. 'Happy?' Jarrett asked.

'Actually,' Emily replied, 'I'm starving. You prevented me from making the steak pudding,' she added, playfully primming her lips.

Jarrett laughed before kissing them.

'We can't live on love alone,' she said reluctantly. She jumped up and wandered away, telling him firmly that she was going to take a shower ... by herself. 'And after that I'll stick skewers through some potatoes so they'll cook quickly, and put them in the top oven, and I'll make French onion soup; we'll have it with the jacket potatoes and follow it with apple pie,' she added.

After her shower she changed into the delicate silk nightdress and matching negligee Jarrett had bought her. She giggled as she went into the kitchen.

She didn't think he'd have envisaged her wearing it to make an apple pie and onion soup.

After a while Jarrett came in and put his arms around her as she stood watching the onions sizzle. 'Ow, your hands are freezing,' she protested as he stroked the top of her arms through the negligee. 'Go and lay the table,' she ordered throatily, then felt lonely when he obeyed.

'Let's eat by the fire,' he suggested as he stepped over to the old pine dresser and opened the cutlery drawer. 'And I'll put some music on. Do you like Strauss?'

She would have said yes even if she didn't, she admitted to herself, but she'd always enjoyed Strauss — especially his waltzes. Glancing at Jarrett, she nodded her agreement.

A few minutes later she heard the music. It wasn't Strauss but a song, a song she'd never heard before. Emily smiled as she listened to the chorus: 'Love in my heart since you came along. Love of my heart, hear my song.'

But it was to a Strauss waltz she wheeled the trolley into the living room and, concentrating on guiding it towards the low table Jarrett had laid in front of the fire, she didn't at first see there was something extra on the table.

'That's why my hands were so cold,' he said as she gazed at the miniature snowman standing on a side plate. 'He's hiding a present, Emily.'

She had to swallow the lump in her throat and blink back her tears before she picked up the snowman and probed him with gentle fingers. 'I don't want to break him,' she explained. 'I'm going to put him in the deep-freeze and keep him forever.'

'I'll put him together again if he breaks,' Jarrett promised.

But her fingers had found the small box and she pulled it out without damaging the snowman. She opened the box and gasped with pleasure when saw the tiny squared crystal hanging from a delicate silver chain.

'Your very own everlasting snowflake,' Jarrett said, taking it from her fingers and fastening it around her neck. 'I remembered it when you told me about the locket you found in the snowman. It was my great-great-great-grandmother's. It's been locked away in the safe for years, unwanted and unloved.'

'I'll treasure it always,' she whispered, turning to kiss him. 'Now you put the soup on the table while I put my snowman safely away.'

Here's a honeymoon memory we wouldn't have had if we'd got married on my birthday, she thought as she made her way to the scullery where she wrapped the snowman in a freezer bag before tucking it into the deep-freeze. *And, really, although he doesn't know it, it's all down to 'Uncle Bear'. I think he's some kind of magician.*

6

A thaw had set in overnight. Jarrett gazed out of the bedroom window and decided he was half-glad and half-sorry. He might be able to get to the hospital later, have a serious talk to Great-unc and persuade him to re-think what he'd done. It would be a huge relief to get that matter sorted and out of the way.

He'd have to come up with a good reason for going alone to visit, though. Maybe he could use bad driving conditions as an excuse, and tell Emily he didn't want to subject her to an unpleasant journey.

He turned to glance at her. She was still asleep — one hand tucked under her head, her hair spread over the pillow, a small smile on her lips. It would have been good to have another day or two cut off from the outside world. Still, it was early yet; they could have all morning alone together. He'd go and light the sitting room fire right now and they could start the day with fire toast, as Emily had called it yesterday.

★ ★ ★

Emily reached sideways to the small table where she'd left Jarrett's sand paintings the day before. She'd decided while making toast over the fire that, as soon as they'd eaten, she'd encourage Jarrett to talk about his childhood. 'How old were you when you did these?' she asked, picking one up.

'Oh, early teens, I suppose. I know I was living here permanently.'

'Was that after your parents had died?' she asked softly.

'Yes, they died when I was fourteen. They were, well . . . I suppose you could say they were professional travellers. Mother was extremely wealthy so neither of them needed to work, though they did act as guides to obscure or dangerous places. Their knowledge and fearlessness commanded very high payment. They were killed in a landslide.'

'Where did you, Desmond and William stay while they were travelling?' Emily prompted when he paused.

'I stayed here and Desmond and William stayed with a sister of my mother's. Well actually, most of the time she and Maria stayed with them at our parents' house.'

He didn't think of it as home, Emily observed, putting the painting back on the table as he returned to his place on the rug in front of the fire. She stretched out her legs and propped her feet on his shoulders. Although she'd heard some of this from Maria, she wanted to keep Jarrett talking. 'You must have gone back there, lived there with your parents when they weren't travelling, spent Easter and Christmas together.'

'They were *always* travelling. None of us really knew them.' Jarrett's voice took on a bleak tone as he continued.

'We saw them two or three times a year at the most. Christmas wasn't usually one of those times. In fact, I don't recall spending a Christmas anywhere but here.'

Emily couldn't imagine what spending Christmas without parents must have felt like. 'What about William and Desmond? Did they come here for Christmas?'

'Aunt Audra reluctantly brought them over on Christmas Eve and they all stayed for a couple of days. Mrs Benson was housekeeper even way back then; she came here just after her husband died. She and Great-unc always tried to make it a family Christmas for us.'

Jarrett stroked Emily's toes. 'I suppose he and Mrs B were my father and mother figures — especially at times like Christmas and Easter. Oh, the parents usually managed to send a tape-recording of them wishing us season's greetings. Or perhaps we heard the same taped voices every year.'

'What about presents, games and

things?' Emily spoke quickly to try and take his mind off the tape recording. 'Can you remember your favourite ones?' She thought of her memento box, in reality a large case where she'd squirreled away many of the games and toys she and her sisters had loved playing.

'The parents used to send money for us to buy our own presents,' said Jarrett. 'You know, I'd forgotten, but I bought that gramophone with money from them. And even though I've got the most up-to-date equipment in music centres, I still use the gramophone and play the old vinyl records more often than not.'

He moved Emily's feet, got up and went over to the record cabinet where he selected another record. He turned the volume low so the music sounded like a ghostly presence in the room, and then sat in the chair opposite Emily's.

'When the parents died, Great-unc wanted William and Desmond to come here to live. But my aunt had been appointed as their guardian and wouldn't hear of it.'

'Whyever not?'

Jarrett shrugged. 'The parents left their money in trust for the three of us, until we came of age. I've got a feeling Aunt Audra thought that if William and Desmond lived here, they'd become interested in Nursery World and might want to invest their share in the business. I think she thought there'd be something better they could do.'

'But they did invest?'

'No. William became a pilot and set up his own airline company. Eventually it went bust, he lost everything and we found him a place in the business. You see, I did put my money into Nursery World.

'I bought the adjoining site, converted the building which at one time had been a military installation, and set up the design studio and another manufacturing unit. I also bought this house when Great-unc decided he wanted somewhere smaller. He owns several properties on the island, so he had plenty of choice.'

'What about Desmond? You said he's part of the business, too.'

'He is now. He used his share of the inheritance to buy a vineyard in France. It didn't live up to his expectations, so he came back and took over purchasing.'

'Did you think of trying anything different first, or did you always want to become part of the business?'

'Always,' he confirmed. 'Great-unc never really treated me as a child. He used to discuss the business with me, show me the figures; he took me with him when he went to select materials and timber, and he even used to ask for my opinion.'

'He could probably tell you were really interested,' said Emily, but she felt sad that maybe Jarrett had missed out on ordinary childhood pleasures.

'I remember sometimes at the weekend we'd go across to Hampshire to a country inn. There was a playground in the gardens; he'd buy me a glass of what he said was shandy and we'd sit outside drinking it. Then he'd tell me to go and look at the rocking horses and swings and see-saws to see how they were made, what materials were used and that sort of thing. We even designed a roundabout together and had it made in Nursery World's workshops. The landlord bought it and Great-unc gave me a share of the profit.' Jarrett smiled. 'I felt so grown-up. My very first wages. The money felt far more real than the money I knew would be mine when I really was grown up.'

Emily had been waiting impatiently for him to finish talking. 'Do you remember anything else about your visits to the inn?' she asked. 'Do you remember meeting anyone there, or talking to anyone?'

'Yes, occasionally we'd sit with a couple of Great-unc's friends. Well, I don't know if they were friends or whether they'd just got to know each other there. They always had their granddaughter with them. I remember envying her; she chattered on and on about her sister and her mum and dad and the things they did together. She had a real family life, something I'd never had.'

'What was she like, this chatty girl?'

Jarrett closed his eyes and a thoughtful frown creased the space in between his eyebrows. Emily could hardly wait for his answer.

'She was a pretty kid — plumpish, giggly but not too giggly. She had brown bunches and I seem to remember she had a pet name for Great-unc. I can't think what it was now.'

'Uncle Bear,' said Emily quietly.

'Yes, that was it. Uncle Bear. She . . . ' His eyes widened in astonishment as he looked across at her. 'How did you know? I've never mentioned any of this to you before. I'd forgotten most of it until you asked where I'd lived as a child.'

'I was the plump, giggly, pretty kid,' explained Emily. She picked up the photograph albums from down by the side of her chair and found the envelope. Then, like a magician pulling a rabbit out of a hat, she pulled the photograph out.

'That's you, pushing me on the swing,' she told him. 'Taken on my seventh birthday. Uncle Bear bought me a present, do you remember?'

'He bought you an autograph book and we all wrote in it. You know what? I can remember you giggling at what Great-unc wrote. You had a crush on me, didn't you? You said you were going to marry me when you grew up. Great-unc said you'd be called Emily Gordon.'

'Spooky, isn't it?' She smiled at the expression on his face.

'You know, I can hardly believe this.' He stared at the photo as though mesmerised. 'I must have been fourteen if you were seven. My parents died in the September of that year. I can remember feeling guilty because I wasn't upset and because life went on just as it had before. We still kept going to the inn at weekends.' He knelt down at the side of her chair. 'Did we meet again after this was taken?'

'No. Granddad died a few months after my birthday, then Gran died the following year. I went back once with my parents and Carrie. That was because I had my copy of the photo and Carrie wanted a go on the swing. You and Uncle Bear weren't there.'

'Were you disappointed?' asked Jarrett.

'I cried,' confessed Emily. 'I was so sure you'd be there, I don't know why. After that, I put my photo and autograph book away and forgot all about you.'

'Jarrett isn't a common name. Didn't it jog your memory when we eventually met again?'

'I used to think of you as Gordon. Gordon and Uncle Bear. It's strange, though. That day you showed us around the bungalow, I felt as if my heart already knew you,' she whispered.

'And I felt something powerful between us,' he said huskily. 'Just wait until Great-unc finds out who you are,' he added, smiling. 'As soon as he's back in his own home, I'll take you to see him. But I think I might chance the weather and drive to the hospital this afternoon. I'll leave my wife doing wifely things like making steak pudding,' he added with a roguish grin. First, though . . . '

Once again, the photograph albums slid to the floor as Jarrett pulled Emily down beside him.

* * *

Much later, Emily opened her eyes and gazed up at the ceiling. 'There's a shape in the plaster which looks just like a gingerbread man,' she observed drowsily. 'Look, Jarrett, can you see it? It's to the right of the light.'

'It would help if I knew what a gingerbread man looked like,' he replied, screwing up his eyes as he peered upwards.

'Like biscuits, with currants for eyes and nose and buttons, and chopped-up cherries for a mouth. The one up there

110

hasn't got a very good mouth, though.'

'Whereas — ' He transferred his gaze from the ceiling to Emily's mouth. ' — you've got a delightful mouth. It's all pink and kissable. And your eyes don't look anything like currants; they're more like stars, sleepy stars.'

'Don't you really know what a gingerbread man looks like?' she asked thoughtfully. 'I could make some.'

'What do they taste like?'

'All gingery and buttery and delicious.'

'I don't think I could turn that offer down then.'

'So it's true.' Emily scrambled to her feet. 'The way to a man's heart is through his stomach.'

'I'll make us a cup of tea. You can drink it while you're working and I'll watch you,' he said, smiling.

'That's what you think.' She laughed and prodded him in the chest. 'You are going to make some gingerbread men. It will fill a gap . . . a gap in your education.'

'I had enough education to realise your middle name should be Pan,' Jarrett told her later, as he followed her instructions for making gingerbread men. 'Peter Pan never grew up; I don't think you will, either.'

'I think it's because Clair, Abigail and Sara are so much younger,' Emily mused. 'I never felt babyish or childish when I joined in their games. I enjoyed myself.'

'Mind you,' continued Jarrett, recklessly sprinkling ginger, cinnamon and nutmeg, 'you are definitely grown up in other ways.'

'Keep your mind on the biscuit dough,' Emily told him primly. 'The ingredients are supposed to go in the bowl, not on the table.' She passed Jarrett the rolling pin. 'Your dough should be ready to roll now. I'll have to make cardboard templates; I can't find any biscuit cutters.'

'What's the egg-timer for?' Jarrett asked in surprise as, a few minutes later, she placed it on the table along with the two templates.

'To see which one of us makes the most gingerbread men in the time it takes the sand to run through. It's all part of your education. And the loser has to do the washing-up.'

It was a close contest, but Jarrett forgot to put currant noses on his gingerbread men. Emily laughed gleefully as she put the biscuits in the oven. While Jarrett washed up, she doodled pictures in the spices and flour that lay on the table like dust. 'A picture of you washing up,' she said, standing back to admire her handiwork.

'I think that's how sand painting started,' Jarrett told her, glancing over his shoulder. 'In George the Third's time, a table-decker was employed to make patterns of flowers and fruit in coloured sand down the centre of the banqueting table. Of course, the patterns were swept away with the crumbs at the end of the meal until one particular pattern took the King's fancy and he remarked it was a shame it couldn't be made permanent.

'The table-decker experimented with various methods of sticking the sand down. Eventually he came up with a successful way of doing it and was employed to paint the ceilings of Windsor Castle. Of course when the islanders heard about it, a craze for sand-painted picture postcards developed.'

'I wonder if any of those early pictures still exist,' said Emily.

'Mmm, there are some at an old manor house not too far away from here. One of the pictures dates from 1850 and the colours don't seem to have faded at all. The house isn't open to the public these days but I know the owners quite well and I'm sure they'd let me show you the pictures and the other interesting items they have.'

'I'd love to see the paintings. I wonder if I'd be any good at creating them? I'm sure nursery-rhyme sand pictures would sell well,' said Emily. 'We might even start a new craze.'

'All right, I'll buy you some coloured sand. You winkle the ingredients for the adhesive out of Great-unc, and I hereby commission you to produce a series of nursery-rhyme sand pictures. I always pay an advance, Emily. Come here and get yours.'

Turning from the sink, Jarrett held out his arms and she moved willingly into his embrace.

'I hope you don't make this kind of advance to all your artists,' she teased.

'They're not enchantresses,' he groaned before kissing her deeply. It was a kiss for her soul to melt into and she wanted it to last forever.

She was brought down to earth by the tantalising aroma of . . .

'The gingerbread men! They'll be burning.'

But they hadn't burned; they were perfect. As she nibbled her third biscuit, Emily chanted, ''I'm quarter gone . . . I'm half gone . . . I'm three-quarters gone . . . I'm all gone.' That's what the gingerbread man says in the fairy tale,' she explained when Jarrett laughed. 'You know,' she added, 'sand paintings of scenes from that story would be fun to do. I can't wait to see the old paintings in the manor house you mentioned.'

* * *

'It's beautiful.' Emily gave a sigh of appreciation as she gazed up at the russet-tiled, stone-mullioned building. To her delight, after watching the news and local weather report — and seeing the roads were clear and safe — Jarrett had phoned the owners of the manor house and they'd suggested he visit straight away.

'How old is it, Jarrett?'

'The date above the door is 1639,' he replied, pointing. 'But the monks built a farmhouse here long before then. There are two stone rooms inside; they were once the main hall of the monks' original house.'

The owners, Douglas and Lisa, came

out to greet them and, after introductions and pleasantries, they said they'd leave Jarrett to show Emily around — and to come to the kitchen for coffee when they'd seen everything.

'You can almost see ghosts of the past,' whispered Emily, when they went through a low door into the stone rooms.

'They call the 'resident' ghost Annabel.' Jarrett smiled. 'She's a little girl with fair hair and blue eyes. Legend has it that one long-ago owner was smothered with a pillow by his son, who was fed up with waiting to inherit. Annabel witnessed the murder and her brother threw her out of the window to her death.'

'Poor Annabel,' Emily said with a shiver, and felt quite happy to be guided away to see the old dolls, toys and dolls' houses.

'These houses always fascinate me,' Jarrett said. 'One of them took twenty-three years to finish, I believe. Just look at the crystal chandeliers in this

Regency house, Emily. The scale of everything is so perfect. Our craftsmen at Nursery World often come here to examine the detail work. That's how I got to know Douglas and Lisa.'

'I can't wait to see Nursery World's dolls' houses,' she said.

Jarrett smiled. 'They aren't quite in this league, but we are very proud of them. And now, my love, I'll show you the sand paintings.'

Emily was fascinated by the large paintings of castles and local scenes; smaller ones of birds and flowers, fruits and trees; and postcard-size paintings of animals. Ideas spun round her head and, although Douglas and Lisa seemed a lovely couple, she hoped having coffee with them wouldn't take too long. She wanted to get home and start sketching out some ideas.

Twenty minutes later they were on their way. Emily told Jarrett a few of her ideas and, laughing at her enthusiasm, he said, 'Hospital visiting's three 'til four-thirty, so while you're putting your ideas on paper I'll go and see Great-unc.'

Jarrett said he wanted to check the air pressure in the car's tyres so Emily went indoors without him and was greeted by the ringing of the telephone.

She was saying goodbye to the caller when Jarrett came in. 'That was Ginny,' she told him. 'Don't worry, it's good news. The hospital sent your great-uncle home this morning and he wants to see us this afternoon.'

A flicker of apprehension coursed through him and he wriggled out of his coat and put it over a chair. 'He can't want to see both of us; he doesn't know you're here. I asked William and Desmond not to mention anything if they spoke to him. Ginny couldn't have known who you were when you answered the phone. She was probably trying to be diplomatic,' he added, hoping he sounded casual and slightly amused.

Emily shook her head. 'She knew who I was. She called me Emily and then said she hoped it was all right to call me that instead of Mrs Gordon. And then she apologised for disturbing us on our honeymoon.'

At any other time the blush that danced across her cheeks would have made him want to kiss her. Right now, though, he was too anxious. 'I wonder how Great-unc heard the news?'

'I forgot to tell you,' Emily replied. 'Jayne went to visit him on Monday evening after you'd seen him. She'd no idea you hadn't told him anything. She chatted about her and Desmond coming to our wedding.'

So *that* must be why Great-unc told William what he'd done, Jarrett thought. Something must have shown in his expression because Emily said, 'I promised Jayne I'd tell you not to be mad at her. She'd no idea you hadn't told him yourself.' She smiled. 'Besides, maybe knowing about it is what helped him get well enough to be sent home. I can't wait to find out if he'll remember knowing me all those years ago.'

'Maybe it would be best if I went on my own today, though,' Jarrett said, hoping he didn't sound as desperate as he felt. 'The side roads could be bad near Great-unc's.'

'No, they're fine. Ginny told me.'

For a brief second Jarrett wondered if he could say he'd rather she stayed at home and make him a steak pudding — but that might make him sound chauvinistic. He'd just have to hope Great-unc would be so pleased to meet Emily and be reminded of when he'd met her before, that he'd have no thought of talking about anything else. But what if he did? What then?

'Penny for them?' Emily asked.

He looked into his mug and then ran his finger around the rim while he thought how to reply. He'd have to say something. 'I was engaged to someone once before. It didn't last long. We both realised pretty quickly we weren't right for each other. But . . . ' He looked across at her. 'Great-unc might just mention it. He's an outspoken old devil at times. Don't let anything he says upset you, Emily.'

'Don't worry, I won't. I feel so happy, I don't think *anything* could upset me,' she replied.

7

'I'm so glad you're here.' Ginny looked up at Jarrett after she and Emily were properly introduced. 'Your great-uncle's done nothing but carry on about some complaint or other from a customer since the sitting ambulance brought him home. Says he's a mind to go down to the works tomorrow and sort things out.' Clearly exasperated, she shook her head. 'I hope seeing you will take his mind off it. He's in the lounge; I'll go and see to the tea. You will be staying? I made a batch of scones.'

'How could I say no that?' Smiling, Jarrett led Emily to the lounge. The elderly man was sitting in a shabby but comfortable-looking leather armchair close to a roaring fire, a tartan rug over his knees.

'Sneaking a small smoke of your pipe, I notice,' Jarrett chastised as he strolled over to greet his great-uncle.

'It's one of the few pleasures I allow myself.' His tone had been irritable, but Emily noticed how his eyes brightened as he scowled up at Jarrett. He hadn't changed much from all those years ago; his beard was white now but his thick head of hair remained the grizzled shade she remembered.

'I've brought Emily to meet you,' said Jarrett. He'd spoken casually enough but, glancing at him, Emily observed a wary expression on his face.

'I can see that for myself. I'm not senile yet. Come closer so I can look at you, girl.' Emily transferred her gaze to the old man, who was weighing her up as though she were a racehorse, she thought in amusement. 'You're better than the other one my great-nephew almost married,' he grunted. 'You've got good hips.'

'You still look and sound exactly the same.' Emily laughed and held out her hand. 'How are you . . . ?' She paused. 'How are you, Uncle Bear? Do you remember me?'

'It was eighteen years ago. He won't remember,' challenged Jarrett. 'Besides, my love, you've changed rather a lot since then.'

'Upon my word,' recollected the old man, as he held her hand in a surprisingly strong grip. 'Little Emily. You were fat with bunches and braces on your teeth.'

'I was not fat,' denied Emily at the same time as Jarrett protested:

'She didn't have braces on her teeth.'

They laughed, then Jarrett said, 'Show him the photo, Emily. Then he'll see you weren't fat and goofy.'

Emily took the photo out of her pocket. 'It was taken on my seventh birthday,' she said.

'You told me you were going to marry Jarrett.' His great-uncle chuckled as he examined the photo. 'Can't understand how you waited all these years then got wed in such a hurry.'

'My new wife has got some good ideas for Nursery World,' Jarrett interrupted hastily. 'She — '

'Hmm. We'll see about that. Know anything about babies' rompers, my girl?'

'She designed and made a pair once.' Jarrett spoke eagerly and, Emily thought, with relief.

'Let her speak for herself, can't you.' Jarrett was duly scolded. 'Tell me what's wrong with these, Emily.' Breathing heavily, Uncle Bear bent forward and pulled a pair of pale blue rompers from out of a cardboard box by his chair. 'We've had a complaint that there's too much material in them. Too much,' he said angrily, thrusting the small garment into Emily's hands.

She could see straight away what was wrong with the rompers. Nibbling her lip, she glanced up at Jarrett.

'Tell him what you think,' Jarrett encouraged.

'OK. I think even parents who like traditional baby clothes use disposable nappies for convenience. And even if they don't, today's washable nappies are shaped to fit inside slim-line waterproof panties. So . . . ' She put her hands in the bottom part of the rompers and gently stretched the material. ' . . . so, you need less material here, to make the rompers fit better.'

'Why didn't William think of that? He's supposed to be our research director, isn't he? He should have realised about disposable or shaped nappies. You'd better have words with that brother of yours, Jarrett. Bah. Disposable nappies. Hope you won't use them, my girl. Still, you've got nine months to think about it. Better not be less. Even if you produce the future heir, it won't count if he was conceived before your marriage.'

'Future heir?' gasped Emily. She swung her head round in Jarrett's direction, but he was staring out of the window.

'You mean he hasn't told you yet?'

'I'll explain everything to her later, Great-unc. For now, let Emily tell you her — '

'Tommyrot. The others know. She should know, too. I'll tell her myself.'

Jarrett strode over and stared down at his great-uncle. 'I thought you'd be really pleased about me bringing Emily to meet you even though we're supposed to be on our honeymoon,' he said. 'But if I'd thought for one second you'd think of telling her instead of letting me explain things, we wouldn't have come.'

His great-uncle took no notice. 'Pull a chair up, Emily, and sit yourself comfortably. And Jarrett, unless you guarantee to keep quiet, you might as well leave us alone.'

Perplexed, Emily did as she was told, and again, looked towards Jarrett. But he didn't meet her gaze. 'I'll just go and tell Ginny to hold tea back for a while,' he said, and walked out of the room.

'Must have upset him,' growled his great-uncle. 'He should have told you, he really should. First, though, Emily, you tell me how your grandparents are?'

'They're both dead,' she replied briefly, wishing he'd get on with whatever he wanted to tell her.

'And your sister you used to chatter about? How's she?'

'That's Carrie. She's fine. Married and living in Spain. And I've three more sisters, much younger than me.'

'I like big families, Emily. It's nice for people to have a lot of nieces and nephews and cousins. I think that's also one of the reasons I decided to do it.' He re-lit his pipe and then began to suck and puff.

The foreboding atmosphere wasn't entirely caused by the fumes from the old man's pipe. Emily frowned and wondered what big families had to do with anything. Maybe Uncle Bear was senile after all? Could he possibly have concocted a crazy idea of a baby race amongst his three great-nephews? A prize for whichever one of them produced the most children in the shortest time?

'I don't really understand what you're talking about,' she ventured after what seemed an age of silence. 'What

129

did you decide to do?'

'Last Christmas, after I was so ill, I decided to make sure Nursery World would continue as a true family concern even after I'm long gone. Originally, I was going to leave everything equally divided amongst my three great-nephews.' His eyes were bright and determined under his bushy eyebrows. Nodding his grizzled head, he carried on. 'But you see, my girl, I want more *future* commitment for the Gordon name. So I decided that the first one to have a son would inherit my shares. Jarrett's already got shares, of course, so if he's the first to have a son he'll become the sole owner. But whoever ends up inheriting, their shares will then be passed on to his son in turn and so on. Like an entailment, you see.'

Emily thought perhaps she was beginning to see. She felt as if an icy snake was crawling through her veins as the implications sank in.

'It was perfectly fair,' growled Great-uncle Jarrett, obviously noticing and

130

completely misunderstanding Emily's look of horror. 'I wouldn't have done it if Hope and William were already married — that would have given them an unfair advantage. But they'd postponed their wedding.'

'Jayne and Desmond were married, though, and Jayne is — ' began Emily.

'Even though Jayne and Desmond are going to have a baby *girl* in May, Jayne told me long ago how they were planning to have at least three babies all close together. At the time I changed my will both William and Jarrett had set their weddings for August. So you see, that would have meant all my great-nephews had an equal chance.'

Unable to speak, Emily watched as he banged the bowl of his pipe on the arm of his chair before emptying what remained of the tobacco into a leather pouch. Then, raising one eyebrow in a manner similar to Jarrett's, he continued, 'I wasn't to know Jarrett would suddenly decide to bring his wedding forward, was I?'

He looked hard at Emily, clearly waiting for her agreement. But she couldn't do or say anything. She was fighting too many emotions. 'You'll change things now, though, won't you?' she said at last. Not that him changing anything would make any difference to how she felt about Jarrett's deviousness, or to her deciding what she should do next.

'I don't think so, Emily. I think everything has ended working out for the best. I suspect William and Hope will now get married as soon as possible. Young Desmond's heart isn't really in the business. So in a way, it's some sort of justice he'll now have a lesser chance.' He chuckled and, leaning forward, took one of Emily's hands in his. 'You and Jarrett will have to work hard to become parents before William and Hope; see if you can produce a boy to continue the Gordon name. Maybe Lady Fate will work her magic again, like she did when she brought you and Jarrett together again after eighteen years.'

'Fate isn't always kind,' Emily said. The words were almost wrung out of her.

'It will be, Emily. I've got a feeling. And if I die before any of you give me a great-great nephew, everything will be divided to give Desmond, William and Jarrett equal shares, until one of them has a son. Then the shares revert to that one. It's watertight; my solicitor made sure of everything.' He let go of her hand, sat back and closed his eyes. All the talking had obviously wearied him.

Emily's misery was so acute it was a physical pain. She knew now why Jarrett had proposed on New Year's Eve. It was because his great-uncle had changed his will. She recalled now, when she'd suggested getting married in August on her birthday, how he'd tried to talk her into an Easter wedding and she'd reminded him that would clash with her family's move to the bungalow.

Then fate, cruel fate, had played into

his hands and given him a reason to bring the wedding forward. It had been nothing at all to do with love and concern for his great-uncle and everything to do with trying to produce a son and heir before William and Hope had a chance to.

Had Jarrett even loved her to start off with? Or had he, when finding out she was one of five children, decided to take her out to see if she wanted a large family of her own? It was obvious his great-uncle had a thing about large families, so even before he changed his will it must have seemed likely that he'd favour the great-nephew who married a wife willing to produce one.

Her fingers reached for her crystal snowflake on the end of the chain around her neck. The shared memories she and Jarrett had made together were meaningless. The man she'd married had no feelings. No. Wrong. The one feeling she could credit him with was determination. Determination to try and produce a son before William and

Hope did. Right from the start he'd been trying to make sure he'd be the one to inherit Nursery World. Oh, heavens. She might be pregnant already . . .

As though from a long, long way away, she heard Great-uncle Jarrett speaking to her. 'Will you pour, Emily?' She looked up and saw Jarrett had wheeled in a loaded tea trolley.

'There's hot buttered toast under this cover,' Jarrett told her. She knew he was looking at her; knew he was trying to make her meet his gaze. But she couldn't. She couldn't bear to look at him. She managed to get through the next hour or so without speaking directly to, or looking at, him. This was accomplished quite easily by the fact he and his great-uncle spent the time discussing the business.

The old man enthused over Emily's idea for nursery-rhyme and fairy-tale sand paintings and promised to make up some adhesive for her. 'I've got a very old nursery rhyme book in my study,' he rumbled. 'I'll look it out for you, Emily, and you can take it next time you call.'

Emily nodded and murmured something. Right now she wasn't sure if there'd be a next time. Wasn't sure she'd be staying with Jarrett. She didn't know whether to be glad or sorry when Ginny walked in and told Jarrett firmly it was time for his great-uncle to have a rest.

'We'll maybe call in tomorrow,' said Jarrett. 'We need to go shopping and there's a good choice in Newport. But how about you writing down the ingredients for the adhesive? It will save you the effort of mixing it yourself.'

'I might need to take the odd rest in the afternoons but it isn't beyond my capabilities to mix glue. It's not exactly a heavy job, you know.'

'Maybe if you like my first lot of pictures you'll write down your secret recipe, Uncle Bear?' bargained Emily. It had been a struggle to call him by the affectionate nickname.

He'd insisted earlier on her calling

him that; said it would make him feel younger. So she'd humoured him because she was anxious to make sure she had something to occupy her time until she'd worked out how to get out of this mess. She was rewarded with a smile and a slight nod of his head.

Somehow she managed to say good-bye and to thank Ginny for the tea, and then she and Jarrett walked out into the cold air. She didn't feel ready for the showdown with Jarrett that was sure to come as soon as they were alone. There again, maybe it would be best to get it over with.

'We'll talk when we get home, Emily,' Jarrett said as they made their way to the car. 'I know I've some explaining to do.'

Emily nodded. The half-hour journey would give her time to think. It would also give Jarrett time to work out his explanation, she acknowledged bitterly as she fastened her seatbelt, making sure her fingers didn't touch Jarrett's as he did the same.

8

'You married me just to try and get a son, didn't you?' Emily accused, the minute they entered the house. She trembled inside, hoping he would deny it. But he just stood there looking at her. 'You knew Jayne and Desmond were having a girl. You heard your great-uncle had made a new will after being so ill last Christmas and *that's* why you proposed to me on New Year's Eve. It wasn't because . . . ' All the thoughts, the conclusions she'd come to, poured out of her.

'I can understand you thinking that's how it was,' Jarrett said. 'I don't know exactly what Great-unc told you about that ridiculous, obscene change he made to his will, but it's clear from what you've just accused me of that he left out one very vital fact. I hope, my love, when you've heard what it is — '

'Don't call me your love,' she said, turning away and walking into the sitting room. 'You don't know the meaning of the word.'

'Believe it or not, I did fall in love with you the first day we met.' Jarrett sounded weary and sad as he followed her into the room. She had automatically switched on the lamps and, glancing briefly at him, she observed that the hollows beneath his cheekbones looked deeper than ever and his face was pale — the paleness highlighted by dark evening shadow on his cheeks and chin. His eyes were dark too, the navy almost black as he rasped, 'Emily, do you honestly think — ?'

She sank into an armchair and put her hands over her ears in an effort to shut out his words. Tears of despair slipped down her cheeks and her hair tumbled about her face and shoulders as she shook her head and whispered, 'I don't know what to think any more. I did think you'd really fallen in love with me. Thought you felt the same way I did . . . ' Her voice tailed away. She swallowed then continued painfully, 'But now I know it was all an act. All you wanted was to try and get a son before either of your brothers did.'

'Emily . . . '

He approached the armchair, but she warded him away, putting up her hands as a silent barrier. 'I don't want any part of it, Jarrett. Marriage and babies should be born out of love, not out of determination to inherit a business.'

He moved to stand in front of the hearth. 'It wasn't an act, Emily. Please, just listen to me. I promise you I had no idea at all that Great-unc had changed his will until William told me at our wedding reception. And *he* had only found out about it a couple of days before that.'

Emily's mind suddenly flicked back to their wedding reception when she'd felt confused by Jayne's chatter and she began to register the significance of Jarrett's words. Mixed feelings surged through her and she wondered if she'd misjudged Jarrett. *Or was that just wishful thinking?*

'I imagine,' Jarrett continued bitterly, 'that after Great-unc found out from Jayne you and I were about to get married he felt the need to tell William what he'd done because he didn't want me to have an unfair advantage. But Great-unc didn't explain any of that to you, did he?'

'No, no, he didn't,' Emily said. And, as she recalled a little more of what Jayne had said at the reception, the ice around her heart began to melt. It really seemed as if Jarrett hadn't known anything. 'But why did you let me find out in such a cruel way?' she asked brokenly. 'Why didn't you tell me as soon as you knew yourself?'

'Oh, sweetheart.' Jarrett walked over to her, knelt in front of the chair and took her hands in his. 'I wanted our wedding night to be special. How could it have been if I'd told you something like that?' He sighed. 'Of course, I should have told you when we were talking about Nursery World and family. I can see now that I was wrong, but I admit I'd hoped you'd never need to know anything about it. I'd planned on talking to Great-unc and getting him to take that terrible clause out of his will. I still intend to do that.'

'I don't think he'll change anything.' Emily shook her head and went on to tell him what his great-uncle had said.

Jarrett frowned. 'The one thing he's probably right about, though, is William and Hope bringing their wedding forward. I'm sure William will want them to become parents as soon as possible. But believe me, Emily, if *we* have made a baby together already then *our* baby will be born out of love. Mine for you and yours for me. Do you believe me?' he added, his eyes betraying his hope. 'You do still love me, don't you? These days we've been together here, you've made me laugh; you've brought a sense of happiness into the house and taught me what it was like to be cared for. You can't deny you care, Emily. And you showed me how to care even more than I already did.'

'Do you still feel like that after the way I doubted you?' she asked.

'Come down here with me and I'll show you,' he told her huskily.

★　★　★

Over the next days it seemed that the misunderstanding — and then clearing it up — had brought them a new closeness, an even stronger togetherness. Any doubts Emily may have had fled completely.

Uncle Bear had kept his word and made up the adhesive, getting it and the old nursery rhyme book delivered to her by one of Nursery World's drivers. Jarrett had gone on 'a secret errand' one morning and returned with some small bottles of coloured sand, a tiny wooden workstation and a wooden tool set.

He'd shown Emily how to create the

paintings, patiently explaining which tool to use for each stage. Joining her at the large kitchen table, he'd created a new sand painting — a heart with their names entwined.

But now, Emily had finished her very own first painting.

'It's fantastic, Emily. Far better than any I ever did.'

'Except that special one.' Emily pointed to the heart painting. 'And, besides,' she said, putting her arms around him, 'I had an excellent teacher, didn't I?'

'I'm going to see Great-unc again this morning,' Jarrett said some time later. 'Will you come with me? He was disappointed when you weren't with me last time.' He'd called to see his great-uncle on the day he'd gone on his 'secret errand'.

'We'll take my nursery-rhyme painting to show him,' Emily replied, smiling up at him. 'Give me twenty minutes to get ready, then we'll go.'

* * *

'I like this, my girl. It's really good.' The elderly man studied the painting carefully. 'The children are wearing Nursery World clothes, aren't they?'

Emily nodded. 'I looked through the Nursery World catalogue.'

'Emily's idea is to use the sand paintings as an advertising tool as well,' Jarrett informed his great-uncle. 'She'll show all the characters wearing Nursery World designs, or playing with Nursery World toys, and we can give details of the items in a separate leaflet. You see, Great-unc, my wife isn't just a pretty face.'

Once again a business discussion ensued. This time, though, Emily listened and watched Jarrett with love in her heart.

'You ought to do sand paintings to illustrate poems as well, Emily,' said Uncle Bear after a while. 'There's one I used to love . . . something about wishing . . . I can't remember what it's called, but it'll come to me. You could show the characters sitting on the famous Wishing Seat.'

'Wishing Seat?' asked Emily.

'It was formed by the great landslip. The Tumbledown, as it's called locally. There are some marvellous old oak trees, too, twisted into fantastic shapes. They'd make a good background on a painting. Why don't you take her there, Jarrett?' he suggested, turning his head to look at his great-nephew.

'That's a good idea,' said Jarrett. 'We could go this afternoon, Emily.'

'Don't forget to make a wish, Emily,' said the old man, as she bent to kiss him goodbye. 'Wishes made up there come true.'

★ ★ ★

Jarrett had slung binoculars and a camera round his neck. As they walked along a path which wound between moss-covered walls and skirted a wooded dell, Emily giggled and told him he looked like a tour guide. 'So tell me about some of the island's famous

146

people,' she said as she followed him down some rough stone steps.

'Well,' he said with a smile, 'Tennyson may have been walking down these very steps when a bevy of female admirers took his 'wide-awake' hat and cut it up into pieces. Tennyson lived at Freshwater; we'll visit his area another day.'

'Oh, yes, I'd love to see the ilex tree . . . 'My giant ilex keeping leaf, when frosts are keen and days are brief,'' quoted Emily as they continued their descent.

Eventually they took a winding path, skirting the many ivy-clad boulders, and Emily felt as though they'd entered a twilight zone; subaqueous green place, but here and there bare trees appeared, knotted and writhen into weird shapes. And all the time the sea murmured softly below. A lonely place, full of haunting beauty and ghosts of the past.

'Here's the Wishing Seat.' Jarrett pointed to it. But he didn't suggest they sit down. Instead, he told her another local tale of how excise men went to a farmhouse to search for contraband. 'The indignant farmer insisted they search everywhere, even the bedroom where his wife lay with a newborn babe. The excise men found nothing. They apologised and left.

'But,' Jarrett continued with a laugh, 'the baby was a doll and the contraband was hidden under the bedclothes. Later we'll take the Smugglers' Path and I'll point out the rocks named after a smuggler called Johnny New who used to sink his contraband there. First, though, let's sit for a while.'

They'd been sitting in tranquil silence for a few minutes when they heard an almost eerie sound of someone sobbing. And hurrying along the path towards them was a young woman of about Emily's age. Her face, apart from a large and angry bruise on her temple, was stark white.

Jarrett was at her side in a couple of strides and Emily wasn't far behind.

'Oh, Mr Gordon, thank God I've found someone. You haven't seen Joe, have you? I fell on the path . . . down there . . . must have knocked myself out. When I came round there was no sign of him.'

'Joe used to work at Nursery World. He died a year ago,' Jarrett explained in a brief aside to Emily, before immediately turning back to the woman and putting his arms around her. 'It's Alison, isn't it?' He spoke gently but firmly over her anguished sobbing breaths. 'Where are you staying, Alison? We'll take you back there and — '

'No, no, you don't understand.' She struggled to free herself and almost fell. 'I haven't lost my memory, Mr Gordon. I'm talking about my son, Joe. He was with me; we were going to walk down to the Chine. I've been down that way; there's no sign of him. I thought he must have come this way. He's only six; we've got to find him.'

'Alison, how long ago did you fall? Have you any idea?' Jarrett spoke urgently, already unloading himself of camera and binoculars.

She glanced dazedly at her watch. 'It says one o'clock. It can't have been long ago. He can't have gone far.'

Emily glanced at her own watch. It was half-past two.

'Emily, listen carefully,' Jarrett commanded. 'There's a white cottage . . . ' He gave her terse but explicit directions. 'Take Alison with you, tell them what's happened and ask them to do all the necessary phoning. I'll start searching along the beach.'

'Be careful, Jarrett,' Emily whispered.

Jarrett nodded. 'And you promise you'll go straight to the cottage and stay there with Alison?'

'I promise,' she replied and, as Jarrett hurried off, she put a firm arm around Alison. 'Come on,' she encouraged. 'We must get to the cottage as quickly as we can. Help me to help you, Alison. Jarrett will find Joe, I'm sure he will. Like you said, he hasn't had time to get far.'

Just don't let her find out what time it really is until I've got her safely to the cottage, Emily prayed silently, guiding Alison along the path.

'I might seem irresponsible, but I'm not. Little Joe has been used to hiking almost since he could walk. He has walking boots made for him, he's dressed warmly and he's even got a map and compass.' Alison spoke jerkily as Emily urged her along the path.

'Shush, Alison. I'm sure you aren't irresponsible. Don't talk now, love. We need to get to the cottage quickly, get everything organised and get a doctor to look at your bruise. Jarrett will find Joe for you. I know he will.'

'The cave. The smugglers' cave,' Alison gasped then turned suddenly, pulling herself out of Emily's grip. 'It's a hole in the cliff, about halfway up. Years ago, there was a rock fall and the rocks formed a sort of path up to the cave. That's where Joe will be. He always wanted to explore it, but it's dangerous and I wouldn't let him. Oh, why didn't I think of it before Mr Gordon went off?'

From suddenly being weak and needing help to walk, Alison now seemed full of strength. 'I'll have to get to him before he falls,' she said as she ran. 'Or before more rocks fall from the cliff-top. His father was killed in a rock climbing accident. I won't let the same thing happen to little Joe.'

Emily knew it would be useless trying to stop Alison; all she could do was to follow where the other woman led and help her as she scrabbled frantically up the precarious slope of rocks high above the stone steps Jarrett had gone down. It was like walking up a playground slide, but there were no safety rails. Stumbling behind Alison over piled-up rocks, Emily prayed neither of them would lose their footing and fall.

She knew what they were doing was dangerous, knew she'd broken her promise to Jarrett and knew they should have gone straight to the cottage for more help. But Alison was unstoppable. And

Emily couldn't really blame her. She hoped she would act the same way herself if someone she loved were in danger.

Time became meaningless as they climbed up and up. Emily trembled with fear and effort. Alison's feet kept slipping; Emily's face and hands received so many kicks they were soon obliviously numb.

'The cave, we're almost at the cave,' shrieked Alison.

And, as she used all her strength to thrust Alison up into the small opening above, Emily heard two voices, one after the other. The first, a pitiful cry: 'Mummy? Is that you? I'm frightened.'

Next came Jarrett's voice: 'Emily, my love, hang on, I'm — '

Then all she could hear was the sound of rocks falling and, before she had time to even think, she felt them hammering down onto her back . . .

Someone was moaning. Someone was hurt — hurt badly? She had to find whoever it was; had to stop them making the terrible noise. But as her breath caught in her throat the moaning stopped and Emily realised the moans she'd heard had been her own.

Then air, rocks and noises swirled around her . . . She was slipping down . . . down, down, down.

It was dark and black and Emily was alone. She didn't like it. She had to find a way out, but she couldn't; there was nothing for her to hold on to. She'd just have to let the darkness take her. She couldn't fight it. Giving in to it, she felt tears stinging her face . . .

'Emily, you slid down the rocks to the bottom of the cliff. You're safe now, my love. I've brought you to the Wishing Seat but I've got to leave you.'

She forced her eyes open and saw Jarrett's face; saw the tears trickling down his cheeks as he bent over her, covering her with his anorak. Was it his tears or her own she'd felt on her face?

'I've got to run and get help, Emily. Alison and Joe are in the cave . . . I need to phone the emergency services; we need to get them out before dark

. . . you won't fall again, I promise. Just lie here until I come back. Emily, my love . . . ' He touched her hand. 'Can you hear me?'

She could hear him, could understand what he was saying. Selfishly, she wanted him to stay; her back, her ribs, her chest and her stomach were hurting, her arms and hands throbbed, but a warm feeling settled around her heart. Jarrett cared for her so much. She could see it in his eyes. His tear-filled eyes.

'I'll wait for you. This time I won't break my promise.' She tried to smile but her lips felt stiff and swollen. He kissed them — a brief and tender kiss. Then he was gone.

★　★　★

'Emily, I'm going to lift you onto a stretcher. I'll try not to hurt you, my love.'

She felt firm arms around her, lifting her; she nuzzled her face against a warm, heaving chest. She could smell elusive but familiar smells: Jarrett's cologne and her own perfume, mixed in with the scent of his heated body.

'Can't smell in dreams, must be real,' she muttered.

'I am real, Emily.'

'I want to go home. I want my snowflake. My everlasting snowflake.'

'She's wandering. The sooner we get her to the surgery, the better.' It was a strange voice. One Emily didn't recognise.

Maybe she was wandering . . . she could feel a breeze on her face. But she wasn't moving her legs, was she? She frowned and tried to concentrate. She made her legs move, yet her feet weren't touching firm ground.

'Keep still, Emily. We're taking you to the doctor's surgery. When he's checked you over, we'll go home. We'll go home and you shall have your snowflake, I promise.'

She knew that voice. Knew she could trust the words.

Emily wanted to sleep, but Jarrett and somebody else kept talking to her.

Somebody, not Jarrett this time, was bending over her, shining a light in her eyes. She tried to close her eyes; he wouldn't let her.

'Hospital . . . X-rays . . . internal injuries . . . concussion . . . observation . . . shock . . . ' The man who wasn't Jarrett was talking.

'Want to go home,' Emily said. 'Want my snowflake.'

'Emily, we're taking you to the hospital, my love. It'll be all right, don't worry.'

She knew that was Jarrett's voice. If he said it would be all right, it would.

There were more people at the hospital, flashing lights at her, wheeling her to . . . 'They're going to take X-rays now,' Jarrett told her. 'I'll be here waiting for you.' She didn't really care any more. She just did what the voices told her.

Then they put her in a chair and wheeled her back to where Jarrett was waiting. Before she knew it, she was in bed.

It was peaceful now. No hands on her body. No voices telling her what to do. Just Jarrett's voice: 'I'll leave you to rest now,' he said. 'But I'll be back soon.' Emily was so weary, she hardly noticed him going.

★　★　★

'I kept my promise,' Jarrett told her when he returned. 'I said you'd have your snowflake, and here it is.' Stooping over the bed, he tenderly fastened the crystal around her neck. 'But I'm afraid you'll have to stay here for a couple of days before I can take you home, my love.'

'I don't see why,' fretted Emily. 'I'm only bruised.'

'Battered and bruised, and you've pulled a few muscles quite badly as well,' corrected Jarrett, stroking her hand. 'And the doctor wants to make sure you don't go into delayed shock.

I'll never know how you managed to thrust Alison up into that cave.' His fingers tightened around her hand as he continued, 'I'd reached the beach when I suddenly remembered the cave, so I turned back and thank God I did.' He drew a shuddering breath. 'I've never felt so helpless in all my life when I reached the path and looked up to see you sprawled out way above me, pushing frantically on Alison's legs. Then I saw the rocks from above the cave falling onto you, saw you slipping down . . . '

His face whitened at the memory and he shook his head. 'Still, we won't think about it any more. You're safe and so are Alison and Joe. They'll be coming to see you tomorrow if the doctor will allow visitors. And I think my time is up now. Sister said I could see you for ten minutes and no longer. You've got to rest, sweetheart.'

But he remained by her bedside until she fell asleep. Fell asleep with her hand at her neck, clutching her snowflake.

She slept most of the following day, too. Though whenever she stirred, Jarrett was there watching over her. She woke fully some time in the evening and complained of hunger. 'I could just eat some . . . '

'Hot buttered toast?' suggested Jarrett, his face alight with relief as he called a nurse.

The nurse helped her sit up. It hurt and Emily smothered a groan. Smothered a groan, too, when a few minutes later she took a bite from the finger of toast Jarrett held to her mouth. 'Easy does it, my love. Your poor lips are twice the normal size.'

She put tentative fingers up to feel them. Then she gingerly touched the rest of her face. 'I didn't realise until now that my face hurts as well,' she said.

'It is rather bruised,' admitted Jarrett, his eyes soft and luminous as he watched her. 'In fact,' he said, 'I think you'll get a shock when you look in a mirror.'

'That bad, huh?'

'Afraid so, my love. But the bruises will fade, so you mustn't worry. One of them looks just like a gingerbread man,' he added. 'It seems a long time since we made those biscuits, doesn't it? We'll have to make some more when you come home, and this time I'll make sure I give my gingerbread men noses. Then you'll be the one to do the washing-up.' And, continuing to talk loving nonsense to distract her, he fed her with small pieces of toast.

'Almost as good as the first meal you fed me with,' Emily spoke drowsily. And, although her bruises hurt and her insides throbbed with pain, she felt strangely contented and cherished as she slipped back into sleep.

The next day, Jarrett's eyes lit up when he arrived and saw Emily out of bed, sitting in a bedside chair. 'They won't let me do any more than sit until the doctor's seen me again,' she said.

'You just do as they say,' Jarrett told her. 'We don't want any setbacks. I want you home where you belong as quickly as possible.'

On Sunday Emily was walking around the ward when Jarrett arrived. 'I can probably come home tomorrow as long as I promise to take things easy,' she greeted him.

'That's marvellous,' he replied, putting an arm around her as he led her to one of the comfortable bedside chairs. 'Sister told me the same when I phoned this morning. That's why I've brought your clothes in.'

Emily smiled. She'd been so glad to see him, so eager to tell him the news; she hadn't noticed the small sports bag he was carrying.

He helped her to sit down, then drew the second chair close and sat facing her. 'It might be a good idea to phone your family in a few minutes,' he said. 'I had a heck of a job preventing them from coming over.'

'You shouldn't have told them I was in hospital,' chided Emily. 'I feel enough of a fraud as it is. I didn't need to come here in the first place.'

'Once I knew you hadn't any internal injuries and you hadn't broken anything, I decided I wouldn't tell them,' said Jarrett. 'But I'm afraid the local evening newspaper got hold of the story. We made the front page in last night's edition. 'Newly-weds in dramatic cave rescue'. I know,' he agreed when she grimaced her disgust. 'I wasn't too happy about it either. Anyway, that's why I had to contact your parents, in case they saw a copy of the paper. Mrs Benson saw the story; she's returned hotfoot, and the phone at home has never stopped ringing. Everyone wanted to know which ward you were on and where to send get-well messages.'

As if to confirm his words, a nurse walked in with a huge floral arrangement, followed by another bearing a basket of fruit. 'There's another gift to come,' said the first nurse. 'Get ready for a shock — a pleasant one.' She laughed as she hurried away.

When she reappeared a few minutes later, it was with the biggest teddy bear Emily had ever seen. 'That's just got to be from Uncle Bear.' Emily smiled in delight.

'It is,' agreed Jarrett, laughing. 'He says he'll come and see you in person as soon as you're home. Jayne's sent the same message,' he pointed out, passing Emily the card which had been attached to the flowers. 'We're in for a busy time, I'm afraid.'

'Put everyone off coming to see us,' she said, reaching across to take his hand. 'This is still our honeymoon, remember. When I come home, I want us to be alone together.'

9

'I thought you'd never get here.' Emily greeted Jarrett with a mock scowl when he arrived the next morning. 'Time seems to have crawled by since I got ready. I kept thinking the clocks and my watch had stopped.'

'I know you're anxious to be home and up and doing again,' said a nurse who walked up pushing a wheelchair. 'But remember what the doctor said. You're to take things easy and . . . ' She looked up at Jarrett. 'Your wife will get tired quickly. She'll need to have an afternoon sleep for a few days.'

'I'll make sure she does,' Jarrett replied, and Emily smiled when she noticed the nurse's blush.

Time seemed to drag again as the nurse pushed her down a long corridor in the wheelchair, then out into the car park. But at last she was sitting in the car. Jarrett put her big teddy bear on the back seat and, after a few words with the nurse, he got in beside her.

He chatted lightly as he drove them home. 'Great-unc will probably be there when we arrive. Jayne says she'll come round some time today, and I've booked an aromatherapist to come every day starting tomorrow.' He turned his head for a second and gave her a quick smile. 'I thought you'd enjoy being gently massaged with soothing oils.'

She'd rather Jarrett be the one to massage her, but she smiled back and nodded. Then she must have dozed off, because the next thing she heard was: 'We're home.'

'It's so good to be back,' she said as they made their way up the steps to the front door, where Mrs Benson was waiting to welcome her.

And, as she stepped into the hall, Emily felt as though the house was welcoming her, too, surrounding her with an aura of contentment.

'You look tired, my love. I think you ought to go for a rest,' Jarrett suggested.

Emily had been home for three hours, and they were sitting in front of the fire in the sitting room. 'I *am* tired,' she agreed. 'Though how talking to Uncle Bear for a while, eating that delicious lunch of Mrs Benson's, and then just sitting here doing nothing can make me feel so exhausted . . . ' Emily pulled a face and sighed.

'The doctor did say you'd get tired quickly for a few days,' said Jarrett. 'Come on, let's get you tucked up.' He helped her from her chair and kept one arm lightly around her shoulders as they made their way upstairs.

Wearily, she allowed him to help her slip off her top layer of clothing. Then she climbed into bed and let him cover her up. She felt the fleeting touch of his lips and heard his whispered, 'Have a good sleep.'

Obediently, she closed her eyes, but

she'd been hoping he'd lie down beside her, not leave her on her own like this. He'd been kind and gentle since she'd come home, yet something didn't feel quite right. There was a sort of barrier between them as well. She was too tired to think any more though; no good fighting it, she had to go to sleep . . .

It was dark when she woke. She stretched, then grimaced at her body's reaction; every muscle seemed to be screaming out in protest against her movements.

She reached out carefully to switch on the bedside light and then glanced at the clock. She'd slept for hours. But this was only her first day home — she mustn't get impatient.

And her long sleep had refreshed her; she could look at things more logically now. Of course there wasn't an invisible barrier between them. Almost contentedly, she stretched again — then winced at the pain. Still, the aromatherapist Jarrett had booked would no doubt help her aching muscles.

Yes, thought Emily, a smile curving her mouth as she manoeuvred herself out of bed and got ready to go back downstairs, Jarrett was doing his utmost to quicken her recovery.

But a week went past. Outwardly, Emily's aches and bruises were subsiding. Inwardly, she ached more every day. True, Jarrett was affectionate and attentive, catering to her every possible need — except her one greatest. Her need for them to be together . . . alone together.

However, he seemed to positively encourage people to call. Every day brought more visitors: Jayne for lunch, Uncle Bear for tea, Hope and William for dinner. Jarrett's cousin drifted in and out, and friends called in for drinks. When Emily protested it wasn't fair to Mrs Benson having to cope with all extra work, she was told Mrs Benson was in her element.

Oh, Jarrett made sure Emily didn't get over-tired, and made sure she went for a rest every afternoon. True, he laughingly escorted her to the room — making a game of it, knowing she resented the necessity of taking an afternoon rest. True, he tenderly tucked her up, as he also did at night after she'd had a bath and changed into her nightdress. But every time his parting kiss was brief and he never suggested staying with her.

She couldn't understand what was happening; she'd seen how deeply he cared for her when he'd leant over her on the Wishing Seat with tears falling from his eyes. And then later, in the hospital, his eyes had shown tenderness when he'd brought her crystal snow-flake and fastened it around her neck, and again when he'd fed her with small pieces of toast.

She'd been so sure everything was all right between them; sure they'd be able to recapture the togetherness of those snowbound days and the days following the shock and upset after Uncle Bear had told her about his will. But the only thing she'd seen in Jarrett's eyes since

170

her homecoming was . . . was what? Just friendliness, she thought bleakly.

She tried over and over again telling herself he was being considerate; that he was frightened of hurting her if he held her close.

★　★　★

Jayne had become a friend and one morning, when Jarrett was busy in his study, Emily confided in her. 'He's making sure there's no time for him to hold me close. I'm either upstairs resting on my own, or down here with visitors.' Emily let out a ragged sigh. 'The only time we could be alone together is breakfast time,' she continued, 'but Mrs Benson brings me breakfast in bed. Then I have to wait for the aromatherapist to arrive and when she does, Jarrett calls in at Nursery World while I'm having my massage. And surely if I can put up with Lorna's ministrations it wouldn't hurt me if Jarrett held me close?'

'I'll have a word with all the friends and relations,' said Jayne. 'Tell them you want some time on your own. And — ' She gave a mischievous grin. ' — I'll make sure Lorna doesn't come tomorrow morning. That will give you over an hour alone with Jarrett.'

Emily smiled back. 'OK, but you come round at lunch-time and I'll tell you if it worked.'

The next morning when she arrived with the breakfast tray, Mrs Benson told Emily there'd been a phone call from Lorna cancelling today's aroma-therapy treatment.

'Does Jarrett know, Mrs B?' she asked.

The housekeeper shook her head. 'He's busy working on some papers in his study,' she said. 'He asked me not to interrupt him unless it was something urgent.'

'Great,' said Emily. 'Lorna not coming certainly isn't urgent. And,' she added, smiling up at Mrs Benson, 'perhaps you could make sure not to interrupt him for the next hour or so?'

Mrs Benson nodded, her eyes twinkling. 'I'll let you do the interrupting,' she said.

Emily got up as soon as she'd eaten her breakfast. After showering, she dried her hair, brushed it until it shone and left it loose. She dressed in a soft green cashmere sweater which brought out the colour of her eyes, and a calf-length cream skirt. She made up her face lightly and touched all her pulse points with the perfume Jarrett had bought her on their wedding day. Then she slipped her feet into a pair of high-heeled shoes and examined herself in a full-length mirror before leaving the room.

On her way past the tall landing window, she stopped to stroke the rocking horse, recalling the fun she and Jarrett had shared when they'd brought it down from the attic. 'I've got to get some of that togetherness back again,' she whispered in the horse's ear. 'Wish me luck, Trigger.'

The horse creaked on its rockers. Emily laughed, suddenly feeling light-hearted. She didn't know if Jarrett had invited anyone for lunch, but at least they'd have the next hour together.

An hour in which to tell him she wanted him to herself for a few days. *After all,* she reasoned, as she made her way downstairs, *he might think I've enjoyed having all the visitors. He probably invited them to keep my mind off other things. The doctor warned us both not to dwell on what could have happened if I'd gone over the side of that rocky slope.*

She stopped halfway down the stairs, suddenly realising how selfish she'd been, thinking of her own feelings all the time. Of course Jarrett would have been affected too. He'd told her how helpless he'd felt when he'd seen her sprawled out above him; his face had drained of all colour when he'd recalled watching her slip down. He'd needed the constant stream of visitors to keep *his* mind off things. *But we'll talk about it now*, she resolved firmly, *then once we've discussed it we won't need anyone to keep our minds off what might have happened.*

Humming under her breath, she hurried down the remaining stairs and through the hall.

'Emily. I thought it was your footsteps I heard.' Jarrett came out of his study and walked towards her. 'You're up early and you're looking much better, too. Let's go into the sitting room and I'll ask Mrs Benson to bring us some coffee.'

'Let's save the coffee until later,' said Emily. She strolled over to the sitting room window and gazed unseeingly at the garden. Now they were alone together and she suddenly felt shy and uncertain, she couldn't think of anything to say.

Her voice sounded croaky when she eventually managed to force out a reply: 'Lorna isn't coming today. She phoned to cancel.'

'Have you got a sore throat? You're

not getting a cold, are you?' The barrier was broken; he rose from the chair and swiftly moved over to her, placing his hands on her shoulders.

'No.' She laughed shakily. 'I haven't got a sore throat. I just felt shy and nervous and . . . ' She rubbed her face into his jumper over the warmth of his chest and her voice was muffled as she continued, ' . . . I felt as though you were a stranger. It seems such a long time since we've been on our own.' He was stroking her hair now and she could feel the steady beating of his heart against her forehead. 'You haven't held me close since the day I slid down the rocks,' she murmured.

His body went tense then. His hands came back to her shoulders and he moved her away from him, but before he could drop his hands she placed her own firmly over them. 'We ought to talk about it, Jarrett,' she said. 'Banish the ghosts and clear the air.'

'The doctor said — ' began Jarrett.

'The doctor told us not to dwell on

what could have happened,' she reminded him. 'We're both more likely to dwell on it if we don't talk about it. Whoever comes to see us is careful not to mention it. Even Alison and Joe didn't mention it after the first time when they thanked me. It's not healthy. It happened, we know it happened and if we bottle it up any longer it will . . . ' In a sudden gesture she moved her hands, flinging them up above her head. 'It will explode.'

To her surprise, Jarrett threw his head back and laughed — a deep, rumbling laughter in which she had to join.

'I don't know what was so funny,' she admitted when their laughter had died away.

'It was the fierce, determined look on your face and the way you described the bottle exploding,' he told her, drawing her back into the circle of his arms. 'And you are quite right, my love. We shouldn't have bottled it up. I tell you what — wrap yourself up and we'll walk round the garden. We'll re-live what happened; then, as you so wisely said, we'll banish the ghosts.' He laughed again, his eyes crinkling as he looked into hers. 'We don't want to chance an explosion.'

So they walked and talked and Emily felt as though they were growing close again.

★   ★   ★

Emily woke early on their three-week anniversary morning and sleepily reached out to Jarrett. He wasn't there but her hand felt something cool and smooth on his pillow. She switched on the light and saw what she'd touched was a note. 'Had some paperwork to catch up on. Meet me downstairs for coffee when you wake.'

Smiling, she leaped out of bed, showered and dressed quickly, then hurried downstairs. The sitting room door was open; she could see Jarrett wasn't in there. *He'll be in his study,* she thought, walking towards it. Hearing the low murmur of his voice she paused, her hand on the doorknob. Was there someone in there with him?

It was way too early for visitors — it would be Mrs Benson in there with him. But, no, she could only hear Jarrett's voice; he must be talking to someone on the phone.

As she started to open the door, Jarrett's words suddenly became clear. 'All I can tell you is that I'm sure you'll regret getting married if it isn't for love. A marriage needs love and trust on *both* sides. I know that from recent experience. Thankfully, I managed to convince Emily I didn't know what Great-unc had done.'

There was a pause; Emily guessed that whoever was on the other end of the phone must be speaking. She knew she should move away. She wanted to but her legs seemed to be filled with lead and wouldn't obey her brain. But then she heard Jarrett's next words: 'It's too early to know if she is pregnant, but I really hope she isn't. That way . . . '

Horror and anger lent her strength. Jarrett *had* convinced her he'd not known about the will; had convinced her he had truly loved her right from the start. Now it was clear he'd just been leading her on while waiting to see if she'd conceived. And if she hadn't, he was probably going to end their marriage because he regretted marrying without love.

'Well, it will only be a couple of days before I know if I'm pregnant or not,' she muttered furiously, 'but I'm not waiting around until I find out.'

It would be no good trying to plan things here, she decided. Jarrett might come looking for her any time now and she didn't want to see him. Dashing to the hall cupboard, she grabbed a coat, threw it on and let herself out of the front door.

★ ★ ★

She had no recollection of actually getting there, but a while later Emily found herself in the botanic gardens sitting on one of the seats overlooking the pool. It was a pleasant spot screened by the profusion of leaves that rambled over the trellised pergola — promising a delight of roses to follow in the summer.

Not that she'd be around to see them, she thought, snuggling down into her coat, then realising with a start that it wasn't her own coat she'd taken in haste from the cupboard. It was Jarrett's and the lingering, familiar scents from when he'd last worn it drifted up to torment her.

She closed her eyes in an effort to concentrate on other things. Tomorrow she'd go back to Portsmouth, look for a job, and stay with Lynne or Veronica until she could find a flat. Be single again.

Having decided that, she couldn't prevent her mind from replaying scenes of her and Jarrett together — all the loving moments they'd shared and the memories they'd made.

'It doesn't make sense,' she muttered. She got to her feet and began to stroll restlessly. 'If he's thinking of ending our marriage, why has he been so loving; why has he kept telling me how happy he feels?' *To lull you into a false sense of security,* mocked a voice in her head. *Until he knows if you're pregnant.*

She slowed down when she came to an unusual-looking tree with purple flowers. 'I think this is a potato tree,' said an elderly gentleman, stopping next to Emily. 'In the summer it grows yellowy-orange berries that look like small tomatoes. But they're poisonous. Doesn't make sense really, does it,' he added with a chuckle. 'A potato tree that grows poisonous tomatoes.'

'Everything makes sense if you think about it hard enough,' Emily mumbled, and walked on until she came to a display of daffodils. Daffodils for unrequited love and also new begin-nings, she noted silently. Well, I need a new beginning; there is no hope for our marriage. No hope at all. The sooner I get away, the better. Portsmouth isn't a good idea, though. If Jarrett wants to find me, that will be the first place he'll look. But there *is* somewhere . . .

10

Emily slipped out of her muddy boots, unzipped her wet anorak and hung it over the old-fashioned wooden clothes-horse which Mrs Sibley, the innkeeper's wife, kept in the small lobby for that very purpose.

People who stayed at the inn were, more often than not, on a walking holiday. Emily didn't entirely fit into that category but she'd certainly walked a lot the last few days. She was the only guest at the moment and was treated like one of the family. The wet spaniel at her side obviously appreciated that; he'd attached himself to Emily the first day she'd gone for a walk and since then she'd taken him with her every time.

'Fetch your towel then,' she told him and, his stumpy tail wagging, he reached under a wooden bench and returned to Emily with the towel in his mouth.

She rubbed his paws dry then went through into the large, stone-floored kitchen to finish drying him off in front of the range where the fire burnt day and night. The smell of baking bread drifted from the bread oven and Emily wrinkled her nose appreciatively. Then she sighed; when it came to it, however tempting the food, she didn't feel like eating. A fact Mrs Sibley had noticed and commented on. Emily guessed comments had been made out of her hearing, too, because one morning Mrs Sibley's young daughter asked solemnly if she could see Emily's broken heart.

Now, the innkeeper's wife hurried into the kitchen. 'There's someone to see you, Mrs Gordon,' she said. 'Demanded somewhere private to talk, so I've put him in the old snug — that little room down the passage.'

'It will be the man from the florist's,' Emily replied as she dried Pal's ears. 'He was advertising for temporary staff to cover busy times. He said he'd phone and let me know when he needed someone, but he must have decided to call and see me instead.'

'No,' said Mrs Sibley. 'It isn't the flower-shop man. This gentleman is tall, dark and handsome and lovely with it. He told me you both used to come here years ago when you were children. In my dad's time that would have been.'

Emily straightened up from drying the dog as though she'd been shot. She felt as if she had been as pain and shock mingled inside and her heart missed a beat or two.

'Here.' Mrs Sibley took the towel out of Emily's hands. 'You'd better let me finish drying Pal. You take a clean towel off the rack and give your own hair a rub. Why didn't you put your hood up? You're wetter than the dog. I hope I did the right thing, letting the gentleman wait? He was very insistent. Anyway,' she continued when Emily still remained silent, 'you know where he is if you want to see him. I think he's prepared to wait a long time. Very determined he looked, to me.'

Emily chewed hard on her bottom lip and pushed her feet into the slippers she'd left next to the range. She couldn't think how Jarrett had found her. She hadn't told anyone she was leaving; she'd just left and taken refuge here in the country inn that held her childhood memories. She'd discovered she wasn't pregnant the day after she arrived and had spent her days — nine long, lonely days — walking and thinking and planning for the future.

She and Jarrett would get divorced of course. Maybe she'd go abroad, go and live in Spain like Carrie and find a job as a florist or with a flower export firm. Her family would be devastated on both counts but that couldn't be helped.

All this ran through Emily's mind before she replied to Mrs Sibley. 'It will be my husband. I'll go and talk to him.' *After all,* she thought, *the confrontation had to come sooner or later; and the sooner it's over, the sooner I can put him out of my mind.*

That was ludicrous, really. Emily knew Jarrett would remain in her mind, remain in her heart, forever. And her heart fluttered erratically as she slowly made her way to the room where he was waiting.

He's lost weight, she noticed immediately. *And he looks as though he hasn't slept for weeks. I can't think why he should look like this when he was the one who wanted to end it all.*

His tension held an almost tangible quality as, without moving from beside the fireplace, he gazed at her a long moment before speaking. Then . . . 'Emily,' he said hoarsely, and she was aware his voice and his eyes were full of conflict and pain. 'Emily, I spent days in Plymouth searching for you. I thought maybe you'd gone — '

'Mum and Dad?' she interrupted harshly. 'Do they know I — ' She'd phoned them almost every day and let them think she was settling happily in her new home with Jarrett.

'I didn't tell anyone you'd disappeared except Great-unc. I thought you might have confided in him; I don't know why.' Jarrett ran his hands through his hair and grimaced as if the movement hurt him. 'It was his suggestion that you might be here. If it hadn't been for him . . . Oh Emily, why? Why did you disappear like that?' He took a couple of steps forward, then stopped when Emily held up her hands as a barrier between them.

'It's pointless talking about it, Jarrett.' Her voice shook and she swallowed determinedly before continuing more firmly, 'Do whatever you have to do to start divorce proceedings. All I ask is that you make sure the divorce goes through as quickly as possible. It's the only way,' she added, when Jarrett made an inarticulate noise and shook his head. But she'd made the mistake of looking at him when he'd made that strangled sound and she knew she couldn't stay in the room with him any longer. In spite of everything, she still loved him and needed him and wanted his arms around her.

She opened the door and spoke quickly, tensely, over her shoulder, 'I'll be phoning Mum and Dad two or three times a week; your solicitor will be able to contact me through them, or on my mobile.' Emily heard him say her name again as she closed the door. She ignored him and hurried along the passageway, then ran upstairs to the sanctuary of her room.

She remembered reading somewhere once that when your heart was really broken it hurt too much to cry. *And it's true,* she thought, as she lay face-down and dry-eyed on the soft bed. *I've just lost the person I love most in the world and I can't cry. And how right it is that everything should end here . . . here in the place where I first met Jarrett all those years ago.*

She laughed mirthlessly into her pillow then, recognising she was almost hysterical, and forced herself to get up off the bed and to go over to the window. It was ironic but the only room that had been available — all the others were being decorated ready for the busy season — was this double one at the back of the inn which looked out onto the garden.

Part of the garden was still a playground, and she could almost imagine the swing out there was the same one on which she'd sat on her seventh birthday. Mrs Sibley's daughter was sitting on it now. In her mind's eye Emily could see herself sitting there; could see Jarrett as he'd been then, pushing her gently on the swing.

Then another image floated before her eyes . . . Jarrett as he was today, and she gave an anguished moan when she realised it wasn't an image, it really was him. She watched his hand move towards the swing to push it.

'I wonder if he's remembering that birthday, too?' She curled her fingers into her palms and dug her nails into the soft flesh. He was probably saying a final farewell to his memories.

'It's over, I've got to face it,' she muttered fiercely. 'I'll go and have a bath, then I'll try to sleep. I can't think and sleep at the same time and I don't want to think, don't want to remember.' But she knew memories would haunt her dreams and sleeping wouldn't stop the broken song of love that played and lived within her heart.

★   ★   ★

Dressed in a cosy dressing-gown, Emily padded out of her en suite bathroom, pink and heavy-eyed. She'd soaked in the hot water for over an hour, trying to dull her senses, and she'd pleaded with her unwilling body to relax, attempting to force it into a state where nothing but sleep mattered.

She heard him before she saw him, heard him catch his breath, and her gaze flew to where the sound had come from. He was sitting on her bed and even through her shock at him being there, she was immediately aware of his misery and despair. 'Emily. Please listen,' he said, as he got up and walked towards her. 'Please, hear me out.'

Emily's throat ached with the intensity of the feelings inside her. She stared up into his eyes. It would be so easy to let herself believe he cared for her. She would have believed it if she hadn't overheard that phone conversation. 'Just get out of my life,' she whispered.

'Not until you've listened. I loved you from the moment you came into *my* life and . . . and for the few days we were together as man and wife you gave me something time can never take from me.'

Disconcerted, she stared at him. He'd sounded as if he'd really meant what he'd said. But how could he? She shook her head.

'What killed that feeling you had, Emily? What did I do wrong?'

She leaned back against the door. 'I . . . You . . . ' she began. She couldn't think straight; his desperate sincerity was tearing her apart. He was breathing hard, the harsh and ragged sound filling the space around her. His face was white and tense and a muscle jerked in his cheek as he fought for, and lost, his composure.

'Oh, what's the use . . . ?' His voice broke as he resumed. 'All right, Emily, we'll get divorced, seeing as that's what you want. But don't expect me to stop loving you, because I can't. It's all right,' he added bitterly as, still speechless, she stared at him, 'I'm going.'

'Why did you say you wanted to end our marriage if you love me?' she demanded. 'Why did you say there was no chance of it working out? Stop playing games, Jarrett. You don't love me and you shouldn't have married me. You said so. You suddenly realised you couldn't live with me even for the sake of your possible inheritance. Oh, yes,' she continued, unable to stop the pent-up hurt and anguish from flowing freely now she'd started, 'I heard you that day on the phone, Jarrett. I know you don't love me even though you almost had me believing you a minute ago. You sounded so sincere . . . looked so sincere. What's the matter, did it suddenly dawn on you that a divorce might take too long and you could lose all chance of inheriting?'

He opened his mouth to speak, but nothing could stop Emily's spate of words. 'It could be years before you're free to marry again. Is that why you came to my room, Jarrett? To try and trick me into believing that you cared like you managed to do before? I believed you that time. Even after I overheard you on the phone I pretended to myself for a while that I'd dreamed it. Then I came to my senses and knew I'd been living in a fool's paradise and I couldn't go on doing so — not when I know what you really feel.' She fumbled for the door handle and flung the door open. 'Now it's time you left,' she said.

Ignoring the door, Jarrett stumbled over to a chair and, sinking onto it, he buried his face in his hands. 'That day you heard me on the phone I was talking to William. Talking to him about *his* forthcoming marriage. He was having doubts about his feelings for Hope so I told him a marriage needs love *and* trust on both sides. You see, at the time I thought you had forgiven me for not telling you about Great-unc's will. Thought you trusted me and still loved me and . . . ' He lowered his hands and looked across at her. 'I was explaining to William — '

'Jarrett, don't insult me by lying. I know it can't be true. You weren't talking about William and Hope when you said, 'I don't know if she's carrying our child, but I really hope she isn't.' You were talking about *me*. You can't deny that, Jarrett, however hard you try.'

Jarrett shook his head. 'I hoped you weren't pregnant because I thought I might be able to prove I loved you — not for any inheritance I might get — but for you yourself. And I told William exactly that. You must have gone before I said it because if you *had* heard it I'm sure there's no way you could have doubted me or my love for you.'

His words broke through her fragile control and hot tears slid down her cheeks. 'And now?' she whispered. 'Do you still love me now after I doubted you again?'

For interminable seconds, Jarrett didn't speak, didn't move a muscle, didn't look at her; and in despair Emily, feeling as though she was in slow motion, moved towards him. When finally he looked up, he was within touching distance. But she couldn't touch him; his eyes looked hard and cold and her whole body quivered in despair. He didn't want her. She'd lost the man she loved.

11

Then, slowly, with hands that trembled, Jarrett reached out for her. He gave a strangled cry when she knelt down in front of his chair and buried her face in his lap. 'Tell me,' she begged. 'Tell me you still love me.'

Tenderly, he stroked her hair and whispered the words she'd longed to hear over and over again. And when at last she raised her face, his tears mingled with hers as their lips met in a kiss so sweet and so true, Emily didn't want it to ever end.

★ ★ ★

'I'm starving,' Emily groaned much, much later.

'Mmm.' Jarrett smiled. 'I'm hungry, too.'

'I'm sure I can smell roast beef,'

Emily said. 'My stomach can, too,' she added, rubbing it when it rumbled loudly. 'I feel as though I haven't eaten for days,' she added more seriously.

'Me too,' Jarrett said. 'Let's go and see if your Mrs Sibley will allow me to eat with you. I had to use all my powers of persuasion to get her agree to me waiting for you. She showed me into the room she called 'the old snug' most reluctantly. Told me she wasn't sure she was doing the right thing; said there'd be trouble if I upset you.'

'I put extra in, just in case,' Mrs Sibley assured Emily when, a few minutes later, Emily asked if there'd be enough food for Jarrett. 'Just go and sit yourselves down and I'll dish up.

'I suppose you'll be leaving us soon, Mrs Gordon?' queried Mr Sibley, over the excellent meal of roast beef and all the trimmings. 'Pal will be sorry to lose you. He's not had so much exercise for many a year.'

'We'd like to stay for a few days, if that's all right,' Jarrett spoke before

Emily had time to reply, and she looked at him in surprise.

'Of course you can stay, and very welcome you'll be too.' Mrs Sibley smiled benevolently at Jarrett. 'It's good to see your wife enjoying her meal. She hasn't eaten enough to keep a mouse alive since she arrived. Getting really worried about her, I was.'

'She's certainly making up for lost time,' commented Jarrett teasingly as he watched Emily accepting another helping of roast beef from Mr Sibley.

'You're not doing so badly yourself,' Emily retorted, pointing her fork at Jarrett's plate. 'That's your third lot of roast potatoes.'

'Did you do it, Mr Gordon?' Mrs Sibley's young daughter asked suddenly.

The potato Jarrett was just spearing onto his fork shot off his plate. 'I, er . . . ' he began, then stopped when he heard Emily's muffled giggle.

'When he was pushing me on the swing, I told him you'd got a broken heart,' the little girl said, looking at

Emily. 'And he said he was going to mend it. Did he? Did he do it?'

Emily spluttered and grabbed her glass of water. 'Horseradish,' she explained inventively, after she'd swallowed. 'Burned my throat.'

'Got quite a reputation for her horseradish, has the missus,' Jarrett and Emily were informed. 'And — ' He glanced at his daughter. ' — from the way Mrs Gordon is eating, I reckon her heart is all right.'

'Right back together again,' agreed Emily, and she smiled up at Jarrett.

'Now.' Mrs Sibley tapped her husband's hand. 'If you'll allow our guests to finish their first course, there's one of my apple pies to follow.'

Emily's fingers searched for, and found, Jarrett's under the table. She knew apple pie reminded him, too. Reminded him of the time he'd made her the miniature snowman. One of the many memories they could share in their newly found togetherness. And they'd be able to build on the togetherness during their time

201

here, she thought happily.

That night when they went up to bed, Emily was amazed to find a single yellow rose on her pillow. Jarrett smiled. 'I told you I'd give you one yellow rose on every special occasion,' he said before kissing her. And all thought of asking Jarrett how, when and where he'd managed to find a yellow rose fled from her mind.

* * *

The weather had changed when spring officially started and a gentle sun warmed Jarrett and Emily's days. They went for long walks and visited touristy spots. They had a picnic in the forest and watched the antics of the ponies. When they visited the famous Motor Museum their thoughts inevitably turned to Nursery World. Jarrett decided enthusiastically that he'd design a vintage type pedal car and Emily thought of ideas for sand paintings and wallpaper designs.

On the last morning of their holiday

they went to a flea market where they bought each other silly little presents and Emily said Jarrett would have to make a shelf when they got home. A shelf to hold their love-tokens.

One present, however, Emily didn't show Jarrett. While he was engaged in a friendly discussion with one of the stall-holders, she sneaked away and bought three silver heart-shaped photo frames she'd spotted. One would hold the photo taken on her seventh birthday, one the photo she was going to persuade Mrs Sibley to take of her and Jarrett before they left, and the third one would be for the baby she hoped they'd made on this unexpected and joyful holiday.

★   ★   ★

Once they were home, Emily thought the house was even more welcoming than ever. Secure in the knowledge Jarrett truly loved her, everything seemed to take on a new dimension. William and Hope got married and, even though they'd probably brought the wedding forward because of Great-unc's will, they looked like a couple really and truly in love.

Emily's family moved into their bungalow and she and Jarrett helped organise everything so what was often a stressful event turned into a time of fun and laughter.

'You know, Em,' Jarrett told her one evening when they driving home from the bungalow, 'it's been an eye-opener seeing what family life can be like. Even when there's been an argument there are no hard feelings afterwards.'

Emily giggled. She knew Jarrett was referring to the way she and Clair had yelled at each other when trying to work out where their mum's favourite armchair should go. They'd tried it in several different places over the last two days. 'I think,' Jarrett continued, 'I love your parents and sisters almost as much as I love you.'

'That's good,' Emily said, 'because I'd like them to come and stay with us over Easter. I'll set Clair, Abigail and

Sara to work. Probably Dad, too. He can plan the treasure hunt.'

'What treasure hunt?' Jarrett said, laughing.

'I thought it might be nice if we had a party for friends and family. Outside in the garden and grounds. We could have an egg hunt and an egg-rolling contest with hard-boiled painted eggs — which is where my sisters will be useful if Mrs Benson won't mind them using her kitchen — and all sorts of other things I haven't thought of yet. That's if you like the idea, Jarrett?'

'Sounds good to me,' he replied.

She smiled. 'I'll start planning it properly in the morning. *And*, she added silently, *I want to make it really special because it will be the first time you've ever had a proper family party.*

Mrs Benson fully approved of Emily's idea and set to making all sorts of delicious party nibbles even, to their great delight, suggesting Emily's sisters come and help her. While the four of them were busy in the kitchen and with Jarrett at Nursery World, Emily got busy on a secret plan. It took a bit of arranging and a lot of persuasion but, eventually, she had it organised.

*   *   *

Emily was slightly worried about April showers but the day of the party was a perfect spring day. As soon as all the guests had arrived (all except one), Emily got Jarrett to announce the start of the Easter egg hunt.

Jayne had brought her brother to the party and Emily swallowed hard when he and her mother took part in the egg hunt and she overheard them engrossed in a discussion about the merits of various wheelchairs — both laughingly trying to outdo each other with manoeuvring accomplishments.

Jarrett had made prizes for the winners and losers — carved wooden eggs that opened to reveal a gift inside. 'Many years ago, before sugar or chocolate eggs were eaten at Easter, people always gave carved eggs to each other,' Jarrett told Emily as he watched her open her wooden egg to reveal the gift — a tiny yellow rose brooch. Emily smiled, happy and pleased Jarrett counted this party as a special occasion.

'What's next, Em?' Jarrett asked. Then he laughed. 'If I sound like a small boy at his first party, that's rather how I feel,' he said and Emily felt a warm glow flow through her. Then she felt a touch on her arm and turned to see Jayne pointing at her watch. Emily smiled and nodded. Jayne had helped her plan the arrival of the missing guest. Uncle Bear . . .

'I can hear a cuckoo,' said Hope, a few minutes later. 'It can't be a real one cuckooing as many times as that. Is it a summons to lunch, Emily?'

'I hope it isn't lunch,' Jarrett replied before Emily had time. 'Great-unc isn't here yet. I knew I should have gone to pick him up instead of relying on a taxi firm. What's so funny?' he demanded, lifting Emily's chin with one finger as she gave an involuntary giggle.

Still giggling, she removed his finger, put it in her mouth and bit it gently. Then, twirling away from him, she demanded that everybody follow her round to the front of the house. 'Bring your camcorder, Jarrett,' she added.

'I'll bring it,' offered Jayne, 'Jarrett will probably forget to use it when he sees . . . '

And, with the cuckoo still calling, coming down the drive, resplendent in an Easter Bunny outfit was Great-uncle Jarrett leading a donkey with panniers slung over its back. 'Happy Easter and Welcome to Spring,' bellowed the old man, playing the part superbly. Then: 'Whoa there, Flora,' he commanded the donkey. And the small crowd surged forward to surround them.

'How did you arrange this?' Amazed, Jarrett caught hold of Emily's hand and pulled her back slightly.

'Easy-peasy,' she said mischievously. 'Jayne downloaded the cuckoo call from the internet.'

'But how did Great-unc get the donkey here from his house? He didn't ride her, did he?'

Emily took pity on his bewilderment. 'He, Great-unc, I mean, slept at Desmond and Jayne's last night. The donkey was delivered to their house this morning. The fee for hiring the donkey goes to charity. I couldn't resist it when I read about it in the local paper. Besides,' she added softly, 'I wanted our first Easter together to be special.'

'Oh, Emily.' Jarrett put his arms around her and held her close. 'Now isn't the time or place to tell you, but — '

As if to prove his point, he was interrupted by a summons from his great-uncle to distribute the presents from the panniers. Smiling, Jarrett obeyed the request and handed a pot of spring flowers to each of their guests.

'The two extra plants are for Ginny and Mrs Benson,' Emily said, laughing as Jarrett with a plant pot in either hand looked around to see if he'd missed giving one to anybody.

'What a fantastic idea,' Jayne said. 'I didn't know about this part of the surprise, Emily. We can all plant them in our gardens and every year when they come into flower we'll remember this lovely party.'

Flora, the donkey, was duly rewarded and her owner collected her for her next appearance. 'We'll go in for lunch now,' Emily said, 'and you can put your plants in the porch ready for when you go home.'

'Which won't be for ages yet,' said Clair. 'We've got egg-rolling, egg fights and judging the best painted egg to come after lunch.'

★　★　★

It was late when everyone started to get ready for going home. It had been a perfect day full of loving and giving, Emily thought to herself, standing at the door with Jarrett, seeing their guests out. And full of happy memories to share.

Uncle Bear was sleeping at Jayne and Desmond's again, and the old man hugged Emily tightly when he said goodbye. 'You gave all the Gordons something they'd never had before, girl,' he growled. 'A real family party.'

'Great-unc was quite right,' Jarrett said as he and Emily went inside. 'But I'm glad I've got you all to myself now. I want to show you how much I love you.'

And Jarrett did just that.

★ ★ ★

The days after the party seemed to pass really quickly. Emily's sisters were now happily settled in their boarding school, her father was in demand for his gardening skills and her mother was better than she'd been for a long time. And although Emily visited her parents regularly, she had plenty of time for herself and her own life with her husband.

Jarrett encouraged her interest in Nursery World and often took her with him when he called on valued customers. 'I just love showing you off,' he told her with the special smile that always turned her insides to jelly.

Emily had worked on the nursery-rhyme sand paintings and they were proving to be very popular. When Veronica and Lynne came for a visit and saw them they immediately demanded Emily do some sand paintings of flowers for them to sell in Flowerbunch and when Jarrett's cousin, Maria, saw them she ordered some for her theatrical supplies.

Emily had also designed an 'old-fashioned with a modern touch' layette and Jarrett had to take on an extra machinist to cope with the demand for it — which greatly pleased Great-uncle Jarrett.

They entertained a fair amount and were entertained in return but Sundays they kept for themselves alone: 'Shutting the door on the outside world', as Jarrett put it, though quite often they went out and explored the island's secret places.

The garden took on a new beauty in the late spring and it became a loving ritual to walk hand in hand in the moonlight every night before they went to bed, Emily happily pointing out every new leaf and bud.

"It is nice to be a flower; but it is perhaps better to be a man, if one can'," Jarrett quoted on one such occasion.

'Especially when that man is you,' Emily told him, and she reached up to kiss him.

Spring also brought nesting birds and, on May Day, Jayne and Desmond's baby, Sally-Anne. Emily had, weeks ago, assured Jarrett she believed in his love for her and, at the same time, had told him she wanted nothing more than to carry his child. Now, the only shadow on her sunny life was the fact that she hadn't yet conceived.

'You've only been married two months,' Jayne had said comfortingly, when Emily, hanging over Sally-Anne's crib, mourned this fact.

'You managed to get pregnant almost

immediately,' Emily pointed out.

'Yes, well, the first weeks of my marriage weren't as traumatic as yours,' said Jayne. 'Don't worry, Emily, it will happen soon enough.'

It should have happened by now, Emily told herself, sighing as Sally-Anne grasped her finger in a heart-rending, baby-like grip.

'Tell you what, Em,' Jayne said. 'Desmond wants to take his brothers and sisters-in-law out this evening to 'wet the baby's head'. He's booked a table at a restaurant near Alum Bay. We've been there a few times and Jarrett came with us once last year. He told us one of the legends about the area. Have a good look at the menu holders and get Jarrett to tell you the legend. You'll understand what I'm on about once you've heard it,' she added.

*　*　*

When they arrived at the restaurant Emily saw that the menu cards were in gold egg-shaped holders. After they'd ordered, Jarrett, speaking in a deep voice, explained the reason: 'Quite close to here, maybe on this very spot, there used to live an old woman called Alice Puckery.

'Old Alice kept an egg on a ledge above the front door of her cottage. The egg was known to wield strange power if Alice muttered over it. The local maidens called it a love-egg.' Emily smiled and watched his face as he related the tale; she loved hearing him talk about local legends.

'A maiden,' continued Jarrett, 'would go to Alice, tell her the name of the one she loved or tell of a particular wish and Alice would chant the words over the egg. If the egg remained perfectly shaped and golden in colour, the maiden knew she'd win her heart's desire. But if the egg changed shape immediately after Alice's chant, it meant the maiden wouldn't get what she wanted.'

'Surely they didn't believe in things like that?' scoffed Hope.

'I expect the maidens saw what they wanted to see,' said Emily.

'Nowadays,' Jarrett added, 'it is said that the ghost of Alice lives on in the menu-holder eggs and anyone who has a particular wish is supposed to stroke it, make their wish and it will come true.'

Hope scoffed again but later, when nobody was watching, Emily ran her fingers over the menu holder and made her wish.

12

Spring had turned to summer and for her birthday on the last day of August, Jarrett took Emily back to the Alum Bay restaurant. She wore the specially commissioned silk blouse with a hand-painted yellow rose on the back — one of Jarrett's presents to her — and a floaty skirt her sisters had bought her. The meal was perfect and, as Jarrett toasted her, she saw the love written in his eyes.

But Emily's one persistent shadow remained. Although she'd made a wish on their first visit here, over three months ago, the ghost of Alice hadn't granted it. She still wasn't pregnant. And although she believed Jarrett when he said he loved her for herself alone, she knew he — just like herself — wanted a large family and she couldn't help but wonder if Jarrett would still feel the same way if she never conceived.

* * *

Three weeks later Emily and Jarrett were godparents to Sally-Anne. Everybody admired the christening gown, lovingly hand-stitched by Emily, and Hope confided that she and William would probably need it in a few months.

Emily glanced quickly at Jarrett. He looked genuinely pleased as he thumped his brother on the back. Emily tried to feel pleased as she congratulated the parents-to-be, and hoped nobody could tell her heart ached with envy.

After the service, there was a party at Jayne and Desmond's house where two surprise guests were waiting for them. Carrie and her husband, Philip, had come over from Spain. 'We went to the bungalow first and when nobody was in we went to Emily and Jarrett's and Mrs Benson told us everyone was here,' she explained to Jayne after her own family had greeted them in amazement.

'I hope you don't mind us gate-crashing. We won't stay long; we've a few more visits to make before we go home tomorrow but I just couldn't wait to tell Mum and Dad and my sisters our news.'

Carrie turned back to her family. 'Your special Easter present next year will be Philip and me making you grandparents and aunties,' she told them.

'We could see you'd put on a bit of weight,' Clair, Sara and Abigail chorused. 'But we thought it was just fat.'

'Cheeky,' Carrie laughed, and when the hugs and congratulations were over, she looked at Emily. 'Em, will you be godmother? And please will you make a christening gown?'

Emily agreed, hoping she sounded as glad as everybody else looked, then mumbled, 'I'll go and see to the sausage rolls I brought round earlier. I told Jayne I'd put them on a plate.' She made her way to the kitchen with a fixed smile on her face, wondering bleakly if she'd always be the god-mother and never the mother.

Simon Hinchcliffe, there as a friend and not a doctor, followed Emily into the kitchen. 'Call in at the surgery tomorrow, Emily,' he said, running a critical professional eye over her. 'You're looking a bit wishy-washy.'

'I was thinking exactly the same thing,' agreed Jayne, who'd walked in as Simon was speaking. 'I'll get Desmond to hand round the sausage rolls. Emily, you come up to the nursery while I feed Sally-Anne, and we'll have a nice quiet time.'

The peaceful room, with all its pretty trimmings and Nursery World furniture, was the last place Emily felt like being in, but she couldn't refuse to go. And strangely, as she watched Jayne feed the baby, she felt more at peace. *I must just be patient and in the meantime enjoy life with the man I love and am loved by,* she told herself, then smiled when Jarrett came in at that precise moment.

* * *

'Hadn't you got any idea, Emily?' asked Dr Hinchcliffe as he passed her a tissue to dry her tears.

She'd done as he'd ordered at yesterday's party and come for a check-up. 'I'd no idea at all,' she said. 'I'm crying because I'm happy,' she assured him. 'You *are* sure, aren't you?'

'I'm a doctor, aren't I?' he quipped. 'I should be able to tell when my patient is four months pregnant.'

'But I haven't had any symptoms . . . and . . . and . . . '

'Now don't worry about that.' It was obvious he guessed immediately what was worrying Emily. 'Women's bodies do occasionally act as normal for the first couple of months or so. I'll keep a strict eye on you, of course, but I'm as sure as I can be there's nothing to worry about.' He went on to discuss antenatal care and told her to book an appointment for the clinic.

'Don't say anything to Jarrett if you see him on the golf course,' warned Emily. She knew the two of them often played a round on Monday afternoons. 'I want to surprise him.'

'I think you'll do that all right. And I know he'll be delighted.' Simon smiled before getting to his feet to see her to the door.

Emily wanted to drive over to Nursery World to tell Jarrett the news, but she controlled her impulse and went to the delicatessen. She was going to prepare a special meal and was glad it was Mrs Benson's afternoon and evening off.

Later, with 'their' song playing, Emily joined loudly in the chorus: 'Love in my heart since you came along. Love of my heart, hear my song.' In between, she sang her own words while she arranged the salad to go with the fresh salmon and selection of cheeses she'd bought, some of which she knew she mustn't eat because of her pregnancy.

'*Baby* peas, *baby* tomatoes, *baby* cucumber, *baby* beetroot, *baby* lettuce,' she chanted. 'And a big apple pie to follow.'

After they'd eaten, Emily knew her eyes must be sparkling with happiness and mischief as she smiled at Jarrett and said, 'Don't move from the table yet — there's one more course to come.'

'Oh, no,' he groaned. 'I couldn't eat another crumb. That apple pie was delicious.'

'The next course will be even more delicious,' Emily said softly, dropping a kiss on his head as she skipped past his chair.

When she returned, she was carrying a plate with the snowman he'd made for her. He knew she'd kept it in the deep-freeze ever since then, but she knew he'd be wondering why she'd brought it out now. 'He's hiding a present,' she said, using the same words he'd used on the night he'd hidden her everlasting snowflake inside it.

She watched impatiently as Jarrett carefully probed inside the snowman. When he drew out a piece of paper wrapped in cling film, she handed him a magnifying glass. 'Take the cling-film off. There's some writing on the paper,' she told him.

Laughing and clearly puzzled, Jarrett pulled the paper from the cling film and held the magnifying glass over it. 'Read the words aloud,' demanded Emily.

'We are going to be a Mummy and Daddy.' He shook his head and repeated it, then looked up at Emily. 'But, how can you be pregnant? I mean I know we — '

Emily nodded. 'We do, don't we. Quite a lot.'

'Yes, but I thought you . . . what makes you think . . . how do you . . . ' The incomplete sentences tumbled out and Emily giggled.

'Come here, and tell me properly,' he said.

'Simon told me today,' Emily explained

as Jarrett pulled her onto his lap. 'And he said not to worry that I hadn't had any of the usual signs because that can happen sometimes.'

'He's a really good doctor,' Jarrett said. 'So he must be right.'

'You are pleased, aren't you?' Emily asked.

'You know,' he said, nibbling her ear, 'I will be when it really sinks in.' Thinking she was probably two months pregnant at the most — because otherwise, surely she'd have known before this, he began to count on his fingers. 'April,' he worked out. 'Is Easter in April next year? Maybe we'll have an Easter baby, like Carrie and Philip.'

'Uh-uh.' Emily shook her head. 'We're closer than that to becoming Mum and Dad. Simon said I am definitely *four* months pregnant. So that means . . . ?'

'April minus two months is February.'

Emily nodded. 'I don't know the exact date but I hope our baby will be born on our first wedding anniversary.'

'We'll have to call her Annie — short

for anniversary,' Jarrett joked. Then he rained kisses all over Emily's face before continuing, 'I mean it, my love. Not necessarily Annie, but I would like our firstborn to be a daughter. A little girl who'll look just like her mum.'

'If it's a girl I'd like to call her Alice,' Emily said. 'Remember the first time we went to the restaurant in Alum Bay and you told us the legend about Alice Puckery? Well, I stroked the egg-shaped menu holder and made a wish. And seeing how our baby is due in February — round about nine months after I made the wish — I think the ghost of Alice granted it.'

'That's settled then,' Jarrett said, laughing. 'We'll have our Alice and we'll let William and Hope produce a boy. William's welcome to inherit Great-unc's shares. I really wouldn't like to become sole owner of Nursery World. It would be too time-consuming and I'll want plenty of time to spend with my family. My family,' he repeated. 'Oh, Emily, my love.'

13

Jarrett took the next day off work. 'I thought we could go and tell your mum and dad our news,' he said. 'Then maybe I could drive us all to the boarding school so we can tell Clair, Sara and Abigail.' Emily smiled at his obvious excitement. She knew he'd make a fantastic dad.

'And,' Jarrett continued, 'we'll have to tell Great-unc and Desmond and Jayne, who'll be delighted for us; and William and Hope, who no doubt will be worried our baby will be a boy and arrive before theirs. But,' he added, 'I meant what I said last night, Emily. I'd really, really love for our baby to be a girl, though as long as he isn't the *first* great-great-nephew for Great-unc, I won't mind if he's a boy.'

Emily smiled. 'That's a relief.'

Jarrett ran a loving hand over her

tummy. 'We won't know until the time comes, will we? We aren't going to let them tell us what sex our baby is when you have your scan?'

'We aren't,' Emily assured him. 'We'll just wait and see. Meantime, we'll call our baby J. A.'

'Jay?'

'J. A. The J for Jonathan if he's a boy and the A for Alice. But Jay's nice, we'll use that.'

'And while we're waiting, I'm going to make Jay a rocking horse,' Jarrett said, 'and how about . . . '

They spent a while making plans and talking to their baby before setting off to visit Emily's parents. 'They'll be so pleased,' Emily said. 'I know they were a bit sad because what with Carrie living in Spain, they won't be seeing much of her baby. They'll feel like they can be proper grandparents to ours.'

Emily's parents were delighted to hear the news. After much hugging her mum, looking ahead, she said practically, 'You'll be seven months at

Christmas, love. I know you were thinking of having another party but I think you and Jarrett should spend Christmas Day quietly. Just the two of you together — '

'Three of us, you mean,' Jarrett corrected her, patting Emily's tummy.

Her mum smiled. 'And we'll have a party here on Boxing Day. I mean for your relations, too, Jarrett. They're part of our family now.'

'No doubt you'll still want to dress up your house for Christmas, Em love,' her dad said. 'But no climbing ladders to hang decorations or put the fairy at the top of the tree. Jarrett and I will see to that.'

Emily agreed to whatever was suggested; there were all sorts of little things she could do, that wouldn't involve climbing ladders, to make her and Jarrett's first Christmas together as man and wife, as expectant parents, one to remember.

But mainly she agreed because she'd got plans for the baby's room. She wanted to start on it soon, and as long as nobody told her she mustn't put up wallpaper or put on paint, she was quite happy to leave any other arrangements to someone else.

Clair, Abigail and Sara were excited, too when, after getting permission to take them out for tea, Emily and Jarrett told them they weren't only becoming aunties to Carrie and Philip's baby but to theirs as well.

'Which will be so much more fun because with Carrie living in Spain we can't be hands-on aunties-to-be for her baby. But we can for yours,' said Clair. 'Right from the start.'

'We'll be able to help decorate your baby's room during school holidays,' shrieked Sara.

'And make things at school for our niece or nephew,' Abigail added. 'That will make needlework far more interesting.'

Desmond and Jayne were pleased when they heard the news that evening. 'We're going to give Sally-Anne a lot of brothers or sisters,' Jayne said, 'but it will be nice for her to have a cousin quite close to her age.'

'That's what Great-unc said,' Jarrett told her. 'We called on him before we came here. I know he can be stubborn and silly about some things but it was so good to see the look on his face when we told him. William and Hope had an entirely different expression when they heard.' Jarrett shrugged. 'I don't think they believed me when I said I hoped our baby will be a girl — ' He hugged Emily to him. ' — who looks just like her mum.'

'It's OK,' Emily said, noticing Jayne suddenly looked slightly worried. 'Jarrett will be just as happy if it's boy.'

'True,' Jarrett agreed. 'Though as I said to Emily earlier, I hope if our baby is a boy, he won't be Great-unc's first great-great nephew.'

'Let's not talk about that,' Emily said. It reminded her of the awful time when she'd doubted Jarrett and his love for her. That was one memory she wished would fade.

Unbeknown to Emily, Jarrett did, during the following months, try to persuade his great-uncle to get rid of the entailment-type clause, but it was no good; the old man was adamant that it stay. Jarrett did his best not to dwell on it and most of the time he succeeded. He didn't want anything to upset Emily and the baby she was carrying.

Though she was a little upset when she suddenly became allergic to the fragrance of yellow roses. He'd given her one after the first time he felt their baby move and she'd alarmed them both by having a sneezing fit.

But he found other ways to mark special occasions with a yellow rose. Like the miniature sand painting he made her for Christmas and the yellow gold rose earrings he gave her on Valentine's Day. 'And very soon now, Jay,' he said, tapping gently on Emily's tummy, 'you'll be coming to join us and, hopefully, your mummy won't be allergic to rose fragrance any more and I'll be able to give her a real yellow rose.'

* * *

On the afternoon of their first wedding anniversary, Emily and Jarrett became proud and happy parents of Alice Emily and, much to everyone's surprise, Jonathan Jarrett, too.

'I think I'll have to go down in history,' Emily told Jarrett as they sat cuddling a tiny bundle each. 'First I didn't know I was pregnant, and then not even the doctors or the clever scanning machines knew I was pregnant with twins. Two babies, Jarrett. I can't believe it.'

'It's probably because before they were born, we called her-him-them Jay, short for Jonathan or Alice,' Jarrett said, and Emily laughed.

After a while, Jarrett went off to phone their relations with the news.

'Great-unc is thrilled to bits,' he said when he came back to Emily's side. 'He can't wait to see them and he's getting Ginny to drive him over straight away.'

It was a couple of hours before Jarrett's Great-uncle arrived. 'He looks like an over-excited schoolboy,' Emily whispered, as he walked towards the bed.

'Uncle Bear bearing bears,' he joked, putting three enormous teddies on a nearby chair. 'I would have been here sooner but when Jarrett phoned to tell me the amazing news, I had to call in at the works to fetch an extra teddy for the unexpected baby. One of those — ' He waved a hand in the direction of the chair. ' — is for Hope and William's baby. That's another amazing thing. Henry Jarrett was born at exactly the same time as your little man.' He glanced at Jarrett. 'Which means I'll have to do as you wanted me to, Jarrett, and get rid of that clause that you didn't approve of. I'd already decided I would anyway,' he admitted.

'I'm glad, Great-unc,' Jarrett replied.

'Yes, well, it wasn't one of my better

ideas. Right, now I've got that off my chest, let me have a proper look at my great-great nephew and niece.'

He peered first at one baby and then at the other. 'Both look the same to me,' he said. 'Can't tell who's who.'

'Oh, yes you can.' Emily and Jarrett spoke together — Emily declaring Jonathan looked just like Jarrett; and Jarrett, glancing lovingly at the baby in his arms, declaring Alice looked just like her mum.

'Or,' Emily said with a smile, 'maybe it's the other way round.'

Jarrett laughed and then handed Alice to her great-great-uncle. 'Keep them all company for a while, Great-unc. There's something I must do.'

A few minutes later, Jarrett reappeared with two yellow roses and then had to take them away again when not Emily but Alice and Jonathan both sneezed.

'Bring the rocking horses in instead,' said Emily, giggling. 'I know you've only made one new one but there's still the one Uncle Bear made. We keep him

235

under the tall window on the landing,' she added, looking at Uncle Bear.

'The Nursery World flagship,' Uncle Bear said, gruff-voiced and misty-eyed. 'The perfect thing to mark a new generation of male Gordons. Oh, I don't mean females don't count, girl,' he added, obviously noticing Emily's indignant gaze. 'But they usually end up getting married and changing their name to that of their loved one. Just like you did.'

'Just like I did,' Emily agreed, reaching for Jarrett's hand and placing it over her heart.

Jarrett smiled down at her and then had to blink hard as she softly sang a few words: 'Love in my heart since you came along . . . ' And he joined in the next line: 'Love of my heart, hear my song.'

THE END

SWEET VENGEANCE

Roberta Grieve

Aspiring actress Kelley Robinson mistakes infatuation for love when she falls for charismatic media celebrity Carl Roche. Despite the warnings of her friends, she believes his promises and moves in with him. But when she discovers how he has deceived her, she is determined to get her revenge. Paul, a seemingly sympathetic journalist, offers to help put her plan into action. But is he only looking for a good story for his newspaper? Who can Kelley really trust?

ONWARD AND UPWARD

Chrissie Loveday

It is 1953, and the Cobridge family is ever-growing. Paula and William have settled in their flat, and Nellie and James's daughter Bella is becoming a rebellious youngster. As her teacher, Paula believes she is suffering from dyslexia. She also thinks the child is somewhat neglected by her overly busy parents. William is engaged in his coronation ware at the ceramics factory and all seems to be moving onward — until disaster suddenly hits the family. How will Nellie survive alone?

THE RELUCTANT STAND-IN

Susan Udy

Kathryn Kirkwood decides to go and offer an apology to wealthy entrepreneur Sebastian Grant for being unable to prevent his wife's tragic death, and unexpectedly finds herself offering to act as temporary stand-in for his young son's departing nanny. When she discovers that Sebastian has taken over the company that her father and sister work for and is threatening redundancies, she is torn between family loyalty and her growing feelings for him and his son, Jamie. And the beautiful but haughty Cassie seems to have designs on Sebastian as well . . .

THE FUTURE MRS. WINTER

Sally Quilford

When Carey Ashmore's friend Jake asks her to pretend to be his fiancée for a few days, she sees it as a chance to enjoy a holiday in the sunshine. What she doesn't reckon on is the brooding but gorgeous Max Winter, a fiery redhead called Rebecca, a drunken aunt who knows all the family secrets, and a deranged ex-boyfriend. Fearing that she's fallen into a Daphne du Maurier novel, Carey begins to wonder who she can trust.